"You think you know it all!"

Beth retorted, eyes blazing. "Well, you don't know anything about me for a start!"

"Precisely." Ryan's voice effectively silenced her. "But I intend to. Before we leave here I intend to know all there is to know—and why you're going to Witchwood pretending to be—"

Beth did something she never intended to do. She lashed out and hit him hard. Then she ran—only there was nowhere to run, no way of escape.

He grabbed her and swung her around to face him. "You need a good spanking," he said. "You'd better be grateful I don't go around hitting women. But much more from you and I'll teach you a lesson you'll never forget!"

Witchwood

by

MARY WIBBERLEY

Harlequin Books

TORONTO • LONDON • NEW YORK • AMSTERDAM
SYDNEY • HAMBURG • PARIS

Original hardcover edition published in 1978
by Mills & Boon Limited

ISBN 0-373-02245-X

Harlequin edition published March 1979

CHAPTER ONE

IT was cold, and it was getting colder, and the snow, which had been an irritation, no more, began to get heavier and thicker, all of a sudden. Beth Linden turned her windscreen wipers to top speed, and saw the wedges of crushed snowflakes brushed aside each second, and the tick-tick-tick of the wipers was a monotone above the engine. It had been so sudden. Had it been like this before she had started off, she would have postponed the journey; but it had been raining in London, and not particularly cold, more of a grey October day, nothing special, nothing unusual, certainly no indication of what was to come. And she had had to get away.

But now, as the grey evening deepened and the snow was whitely round the car, and she had left the main road, she began to feel uneasy. She had no idea if she was near a village. Names on a map were all very well, but sometimes they could be a scatter of houses, a hamlet, no more. There were twenty more miles to Witchwood, and she had planned to arrive at six. It looked as if she might be delayed. Beth began to mentally look out for an inn or an hotel, anywhere she might stay the night, but with the leaving of the road, it seemed as if she might have left civilisation behind as well.

It was dark now. The road shone back, reflecting in her headlights, and all was white and eerie. The trees at the side were no help; they only served to accentuate the loneliness. Then she was made sharply aware of something she had subconsciously tried to ignore: the wheels of the car were clogging up, getting slower. She revved up, the engine whirred, and she felt heavy, as if she were part of the car, as if the effort were hers too.

A gentle sliding, a skidding, and the car slewed across the narrow road and came to a halt, inches away from a whitely shining hedge. For a moment she panicked, then her natural common sense asserted itself and calmness took over. Panic wouldn't help; she was only about three miles away from a major road, certainly nothing to worry about. She opened the door and the flurry of snow rushed in, deadly and white and cold. She closed it again and switched off the engine. Then she reached in the back, lifted her coat up, and put it on. What did she do now?

She waited a moment, then switched on the engine, put the car into reverse gear, and felt it begin to move. Cautiously and with extreme slowness she regained her position on the road. And then, when she was about to change gear again, into first, there came a whirring and a coughing, and the car stopped.

It was then that she began to feel frightened. The world was a white blur outside, and all was silent. Opening the door, taking a deep breath, she stood outside and bent to look at the front wheels. They were clogged with snow. Then into the deadly silence came the sound of a car. Nearer and nearer it came, but she could see nothing for the blinding, blanketing snowflakes, thicker with every second that passed.

Then she saw the car and began her slithering run towards it, waving her arms to stop the driver before he—or she—could collide with her own car. The car stopped, she saw a man get out and come towards her, and felt relief. At least she was no longer alone. . . .

'What the hell's going on?' A furious voice halted

her in her tracks. Bewildered, she waited to see who had spoken. A tall man stopped in front of her, a tall, well-built husky figure clad in thick jacket and jeans. 'What have you stopped for?' It seemed a ridiculous question. What on earth did he imagine—that she had paused to admire the scenery?

'My car's stuck,' she answered. He muttered something under his breath, then:

'Are you alone?' he asked.

'Yes. Are you?' He ignored that, brushed past her, and stalked over to her car and slid in. Beth followed him, shivering, her teeth chattering with the cold. He was switching on, listening to the vain whine of her engine.

'Damn and blast it,' he said. 'You've really done it, haven't you?' and unfolded himself from the driving seat. Beth bit her lip.

'Won't it go?' she asked.

'No, it won't. And you've effectively blocked the road as well.' He glared down at her, and she sensed an explosive temper, barely controlled. Her heart sank.

'What shall I do?'

'There's not a lot you can do, you silly bitch,' he answered swiftly. 'Have you seen the weather?' He looked round him. 'God, give me strength!'

'We're only a few miles from the——'

'A few miles—precisely. How far do you think we'd walk in this?' he glared at her again, then ran his hands through snow covered hair. 'We're stuck, woman—stuck!'

'I'm sorry,' she said, because it seemed the only thing to say.

'Well, *that's* a relief!' his tone was laced with sarcasm. 'You're sorry! Can we all go home now?'

Beth was normally easy-going, even-tempered, and calm. Her temper, usually kept well in check, rose suddenly. 'Don't talk so stupid,' she retorted. 'It's not *my* fault I——'

'Don't tell me I'm stupid,' he cut in. 'I was doing fine till you stopped me. I'd have got through if it wasn't for this old banger blocking the way——'

'It's not an old banger!' she shot back, 'and if I hadn't waved, you'd have crashed into it——'

'I'd have stopped. I saw you, you know. I thought you'd had an accident.' He looked round. 'We can't stay here.'

'Then what do you suggest we do?'

'Get out of it.'

'How?'

He looked at her. 'Apart from pushing your car, which is getting more impossible the longer we stand here arguing, there's only one thing to do—find somewhere to shelter.'

Her heart sank. 'You mean—to *stay*?'

'What else? You've stopped, so have I. The weather's getting worse—or hadn't you noticed?'

'Don't blame *me* for the weather. How much further would you have got?'

'How the hell do I know? I didn't get the chance, did I? We can't stand here. Get in your car.' He took her arm and she felt herself being pushed towards her Mini, into the front passenger seat. The door closed, then the man was in the driving seat. He switched on the interior light and looked at her. 'We won't move again tonight,' he said. 'Accepting that, the next thing we have to think about is—where will we stay? Yours or mine?'

'Oh,' she said.

'It's quite simple,' he went on, and she watched him as he spoke. The snow was melting from his hair, and it was now dark. His face was dark too—with temper. Under normal circumstances, she realised, he would be good-looking, in a lean, casual way, but his furious temper lent him an air that effectively concealed his features. 'We'll freeze if we don't decide, and fast. Now shut up, and let me think. Have you a map?'

She produced it silently and he took it from her, and studied it. 'Hmm. Three miles, approximately—that means——' his fingers jabbed the page, 'we're here.' There was silence for a moment. Then: 'Hell and damnation!' He glared at her stonily. 'You'd better wait here.'

'Where—are you going?' she whispered.

'There's an old cottage near here—or should be. I'll find it.' He was gone. Beth folded up the map and waited, shivering. She had been alone, and understandably nervous, then Sir Galahad had ridden up out of the darkness to her rescue—more or less. The only trouble was, she wasn't sure if she wanted to be rescued by him. She didn't have much choice. Three minutes later her car door was wrenched open, and the errant knight's deep voice said: 'Come on, time to move. Grab the *essentials*, we're moving.' The next minute was a blur of activity. He was writing something on a sheet of paper taken from a notebook in his pocket, then he vanished, to return moments later carrying a flask.

'Ready?' he said.

'Yes.' She had her bag; that was all she needed. He also carried what looked like a couple of blankets, and a torch.

'This way.' He struck out through a gap in the hedge, and Beth followed.

He pushed open the creaking door of the derelict cottage and went in. Beth followed, wrinkling her nose at the smell of damp and mildew. 'Beggars can't be choosers,' he said, seeing her expression in the torch's gleam.

'I'd rather stay in my car,' she said.

'Don't be stupid,' was the crisp reply. He flung the blankets over an aged bench and knelt in front of the fireplace, his torch probing the dark like a yellow knife. 'I'm going to light a fire,' he said. 'You do know how to make firelighters out of newspapers, I hope?'

'I'm not *entirely* stupid,' she retorted.

'Right.' He handed her a newspaper from beneath the blankets. 'Today's *Times*. Save one sheet to crumple up. I'm going to search for wood.' And he vanished with the torch, leaving her in the pitch darkness. Beth wondered, as she unfolded the newspaper by touch, what he had written, and when he returned several minutes later, carrying an assortment of planks and pieces of wood, she asked him.

'Directions to this place,' he answered her, 'and I stuck them on my car windscreen—inside—for any other poor fool who gets stuck behind us.' He began breaking the wood up with the heel of his shoe, cracking down as he balanced it against the edge of the fireplace. 'Any more questions?'

There was none. Beth sensed a man who would take control of any situation—a survivor—the right person to be stranded with, certainly, but did he have to be so aggressive? She continued making paper spills, because it seemed the wisest thing to do. It was freezing cold, and even with her coat, her body was beginning to feel numb.

He took them from her, laid the crumpled sheet in the

hearth, piled on her spills, and then the wood. Lighting a match, he shielded it, then put it to the paper. She knew it would burn. It wouldn't dare do otherwise, and it did.

It was almost worth everything to see the yellow flames leaping, catching the wood moments later, to hear the satisfactory crackle as the pieces caught hold and began to burn. He stood up and dusted his hands. 'That's better.' Then he looked at her. 'Have you any food in your car?'

Beth had to think, to force herself. The cold was seeping into her bones, the fire not yet warming enough to dispel it, and it was an effort to think.

'Yes. Some sandwiches and a flask of coffee.'

'Where?'

'In the—glove compartment.'

'Right. I've got some too. Feed the fire.' He was gone. She knelt in front, warming her hands in the welcoming flames, and life began to return to her limbs. She looked around her. It was a bare room, dusty-floored, with a threadbare carpet that the late occupants had clearly considered not worth removing. She wondered who they had been.

There was a flurry of snow as the door opened, cold air rushed in, then it was shut again. The man laid several things on the floor and crouched down beside her. 'We won't starve,' he said.

'That's a relief.' She couldn't help the sarcasm.

He frowned at her. 'You're a lippy creature,' he remarked. 'Considering it's your fault I'm stuck here——'

'It's a pity *you* weren't in front,' she retorted. 'Then you'd have no doubt reached your destination by now. I'd have managed.'

'How? By sitting in your car and freezing? Sure.'

'Don't be stupid! I'd have used the heater——'

'Until the battery ran down—or the petrol ran out. Yes, you'd have managed all right—to get yourself frozen.'

'Are we going to sit here swapping insults all night?' she asked.

'No. We're going to get warm, and then sleep. Before we sleep, we'll eat some of the food. We'll save the rest in case we're stranded for longer than overnight——'

'Which God forbid,' she said fervently.

'Amen to that. But it could happen.'

She stared at him. And for the first time, something of the reality of the situation began to seep into her. 'You mean——' she began.

'I mean it's possible. Anything's possible. This is a freak snowstorm—and we're right bang in the middle of it. As are dozens of others, probably. Listen, Miss—what's your name anyway?'

'Beth Linden.'

'Linden? Where are you going?'

'Does it matter? What's *your* name?'

'Call me Ryan.'

'Is that your first or second name?'

'Christian name.'

'Why did you query my surname?' she stared at him.

'Because it's unusual, and because I'm going to a house whose owner has the same surname. Where are you going?'

'It's none of your business.'

'I've just made it my business.'

She didn't like him. He was large, and aggressive, and prickly, and she objected to being questioned as though he had the right to do so. She flung a stick on the fire, watched it catch fire and begin to blaze, then she stared at him. 'All right,' she said. 'What's the name of this house you're going to?'

'Witchwood.' She should have known. She closed her eyes.

'And that's where you're going too.' It was hardly a question, more a statement.

'Yes.' She said it very quietly.

'My God.' He took her chin, and turned her to face him. 'Why? Who are you?'

'I don't—please, you're hurting me——' She was frightened of this man, and she was alone with him. That was worse. Her eyes met his and in them she saw the hardness, the questioning, and she was unable to look away.

'Tell me,' he said.

'He—Mr Linden—is my grandfather.'

He released her abruptly, and the anger was only too obvious. 'No,' he said, loudly. 'No—you're lying.'

'I'm not. Why do you stare at me?' Her voice was shaky with fear.

'I want to look at you. To see who you really are,' he answered, and his voice shook with anger.

'I've already told you.' She spaced the words out, evenly and calmly.

'He has no granddaughter.'

'Are you a relative?'

'No.'

'Then—forgive my impertinence——' she didn't try to hide the sarcasm. She was completely fed up with him, 'but what do *you* know about who is or isn't related to him?'

'He and my grandfather are—were—old friends. I've been visiting the house regularly for the past eight years, and he has never—but never—mentioned you.' He gave her a hard level look. 'And that, believe me, gives me the right to doubt you.'

It was difficult, of course. She had no intention of telling him the full story. Yet he was not a man to be fobbed off or ignored. Why, oh, why did she have to meet him? A friendly AA man, a cottager who would have welcomed her in for shelter, anyone but this questioning, hard man. She shrugged.

'Can we eat?' she said.

'No. Not until we've sorted out who you are.'

'I can eat *my* sandwiches,' she snapped.

'No, you can't.'

'What?' she stared at him. 'Who are you——'

'I've found us shelter. I'm in charge. We eat when I say, not before. We don't know how long we'll be here——'

'Don't be so dramatic,' she said scornfully. 'I'm sure you think you're a big man, but you don't impress me——' he cut off her words by standing up, pulling her to her feet, and over to the door. Then he opened it and pushed her outside. Beth gasped and caught her breath at the ferocity of the blizzard, the blinding icy sleety snow that surrounded and covered her within seconds. It was already inches deep, piling up against the wall, smothering inwards. He dragged her in and slammed the door. Wide-eyed, frightened, wordless, she stared at him.

'Now,' he grated. 'Now, argue about food—and about how long we'll be here.'

She wiped her face, rubbed her soaking hair, then took off her coat and shook it. She was shivering with cold. 'Get by the fire. Dry your coat, then sit down,' he commanded.

She went and held her coat in front, seeing the steam

rise from it as he flung on more pieces of wood to crackle and burn. 'I'm going to go through the house to see if there's anything else I can burn,' he said. 'Are you coming with me or staying here?'

'I'll stay here.'

'Can I trust you not to touch the food—not even your own?'

'Yes.'

Without a word, he left her. The shadows danced in the corners, and she heard him moving about upstairs, and she knew now that she would not have liked to be alone. She would not have liked it at all. The cottage wasn't large, but it was old, and there were creaks from above, and a strange deadening pressure from outside, as if the snow might stifle them. She went over to the window, rubbed the pane, and peered through. Whiteness filled the air, a swirling reckless whiteness, accompanied by the faint wind sounds, the eerie moaning that echoed down the chimney as well, making the wood spurt and spark in protest. And yet—despite the aggression, the insults, the disbelief—she couldn't imagine the man Ryan being afraid of anything. Nor could she imagine him being unable to cope with any situation.

He was coming down the stairs, but not into the room. She heard his footsteps recede, a door banged, then silence. For a horrible moment she thought he had walked out and left her, and even though she knew it was impossible, yet the idea was fearful. She began to count the seconds.

'We're all right for fuel.' He was back, crossing to the fire, crouching down, his face and hands dusty and smudged. 'There's a coalshed at the back with enough bits and coal dust to keep a fire going for a couple of days, and there are wooden banisters, which, if necessary,

I shall break down and burn.' And he would too; she didn't doubt that.

'I'm sorry,' she said.

He looked surprised. 'What for? The house is derelict —no one will miss the banisters. There are wooden cupboards as well.'

'Not that. For accusing you of being dramatic. The weather is worse than I thought.'

'Now you're talking sensibly. I've lived in the Antarctic for several months, and I've encountered conditions far worse than these, when your gloves would freeze to your fingers if you got them damp and your fingers could drop off and you wouldn't even know until you got into the warm and thawed out—but I'll tell you this. This is the worst weather I've ever seen in England. I'm not joking. In about half an hour I'm going out to see if there are any more cars on the road. You'd have frozen if you'd stayed in yours tonight.' He looked at his watch. 'Right. We'll have one coffee each and a sandwich. Then we'll organise the sleeping arrangements.'

Numbly, Beth passed him her flask, opened the packet of sandwiches and waited for further orders. It seemed better not to say anything at all. She had a suspicion, as yet unformed, at the back of her mind, with regard to the 'sleeping arrangements', but she dared not ask. It seemed that it might be better not to know, at least not until she had eaten.

He passed her the cup of coffee, unscrewed the cup from his own flask, and poured himself out a cup. In silence they ate and drank. One sandwich, one cup of coffee. She looked longingly at the others, then put them away.

'Cigarette?'

'I don't smoke, thank you.' He squinted in the light from the fire at his packet.

'I've got five left. One now, then I'll put them away.' He lit it and put the packet on the mantelpiece. 'While I'm gone out looking, warm the blankets by the fire. Have you any cushions in your car?'

She had to think. 'No. But I've got those furry seat covers on the front two seats——'

'Detachables?'

'Yes.'

'I'll get them. Anything else useful you can think of?'

'What about extra clothes? I've got a couple of sweaters in my suitcase——'

'*Now* you're using your brains.'

'But you said only essentials——'

'That was before we knew we'd be sleeping here. It could have passed. It hasn't. We're stuck.'

'I'd better come with you, then. Won't you need your own case?'

'I travel light. Mine are at Witchwood. I leave them there.'

Beth let that sink in for a moment. She didn't want to get on *that* subject again. Hastily, she said: 'I've got a chunky sweater you might get on at a pinch——'

He laughed. 'I doubt it. I'll fetch your case. Got your keys?'

'It's not in the boot—it's on the back seat.'

'Okay. I'm going. Get the blankets warmed.' The icy air swept in as he opened the door, then he was gone. Beth stood up, shook out the blankets, and held them not too near, to warm.

He was gone for ages. Her vivid imagination supplied the images she dared not voice. What if he had fallen? Or got lost? He had left the torch, and it was switched off. When twenty minutes had passed, she was about to set off in search when there was a banging at the door and she ran to open it. He nearly fell in, loaded up, snow-covered, and bringing in the icy air with him. 'Good grief,' he said, 'your case weighs a ton!' He put it down, then removed his coat, under which was bundled her precious sheepskin covers. 'Take those,' he said. 'Set them out by the fire. We'll lie on them and use some sweaters of yours as pillows.' He rubbed the snow from his black hair. 'There are no other cars, thank God. We're stuck with each other. And I'd better tell you now, so we can argue it out before we settle down to sleep. To keep warm, we'll have to lie side by side. Any comments?'

CHAPTER TWO

THE faint suspicion was now confirmed. Wordlessly, Beth took her case and knelt down to open it. She knew quite well that what he said was sensible. It just didn't make her feel any easier about it.

'Lost your tongue? You had enough to say before. And don't think I've forgotten about Witchwood. We'll discuss *that* in the morning.'

She looked up at him. 'You can hardly expect me to be overjoyed at the idea of sleeping with a strange man,' she said.

'No. True. And I appreciate your feelings, but you'll be quite safe. Does that reassure you?'

'You'd hardly say otherwise, would you?' She bit her lip. 'I know there's no choice. I'm not that stupid, I've read enough about survival in the extreme cold to know about warmth from human bodies. But——'

'But what? All men aren't sex maniacs. I'm not, anyway. I don't know about the kind you've met.' He laid his coat before the fire. 'I have no intentions of trying to seduce you.'

She had heard that one before. She had heard all the variations of all the passes in the world, but she had never been trapped in a snowbound house alone with a man before, and a stranger at that. She knew how to deal with men. She had learnt to early, when, at the age of sixteen, her puppy fat had vanished, and she had emerged a beautiful young woman. Now she was twenty, and knew the right answers, the right evasions, and she

was admired by several besotted young men, but she
had never given her heart, or her body, to any of them,
because none of them appealed to her enough. Her
friends said she was too choosy, but Beth knew different.
One day, *the* man would come along and she would look
at him, and she would know. Until that day, she preferred to wait. She stood up and passed him the large
sweater. 'You'd better see if you can get that on,' she
said.

'Thanks. You haven't answered me.'

'You didn't ask me a question. You assured me you
weren't going to try and seduce me. I've heard that before.' A flicker of bitterness touched her mouth for a
moment, and she looked at him in the flickering firelight,
and saw—very briefly—something in his eyes, and
looked away. A sigh escaped her.

'I won't say it again, because I can see you wouldn't
believe me if I did. When morning comes, you'll know I
meant what I said, though.' He pulled the sweater over
his head, and she heard his muffled voice: 'Oh God,
I'm stuck!'

'Wait—here.' She eased it off, and he smiled.

'Sorry, no go. Pity—it looks warm.' He shrugged. 'I'm
a bit larger than you.' That was an understatement. He
was tall, well over six feet, and broadly built. She hadn't
really thought it would fit him, but it seemed worth a
try. She stared at him. He was powerful too. He was far
stronger than she was. She felt herself shiver.

'Cold?' he asked.

'No. Yes—but it wasn't that.'

'You're frightened of me?'

'Of course—not.'

'You don't need to be. There is no way I would use my
strength against a woman.' He ran his fingers through

his damp hair. 'Oh, what the hell!' he glared down at her. 'My God, I don't know what kind of man you go out with——'

'Normal ones,' she answered.

'Yes? It sounds like it—come off it. Do you have to fight them off all the time?'

'More or less.'

'Then this should be a change—and a rest—for you.' He turned away as if exasperated. 'Let's get the bed made up. I'm tired—I've been driving since six this morning. I'll be fast asleep in two minutes.'

She hoped he would, but she doubted it. He spread out the seat covers side by side, and she passed him cardigans and sweaters, which he folded carefully. Without looking up, he said: 'The loo's at the back of the house. The bad news is—it's outside. The good news is—it's sheltered by the wall. You shouldn't get more than about a hundredweight of snow down your neck. Goodnight.' And he lay down and pulled his half of the two blankets over him. Beth looked at him for a moment, then took the torch and went out.

When she returned, only minutes later, he was fast asleep.

She awoke in the middle of the night to hear the wind howling round the house. The room was cold, and so was she. She realised why when she saw the blankets that he had pulled from her, presumably when turning in his sleep. Shivering, she tried very cautiously and gently to retrieve her share, and he stirred and mumbled something, then was still. She edged closer until she was lying behind him. At least he was warm. She knew the sense of what he had said before. The only thing she hadn't allowed for in her worries was that he would take her blankets from her. Very, very slowly she began to inch the coverings her way, holding her breath, pausing at the slightest movement on his part, until she had nearly succeeded, when——

'What the——' he sat up abruptly and glared at her. '*What* are you trying to *do*?'

'The blankets—I'm frozen,' she whispered. 'I'm sorry, but you'd taken them——'

'Mmm,' he mumbled, already, it seemed, exhausted with the effort of speaking, and he lay down. 'Help yourself. Tuck it in at your back firmly and lie as close as you can—just let me go to——' his words tailed off. Beth reached behind her, tucked the blankets under her, snuggled closer, because he really was warm, and already asleep again, and she was safe, and minutes later she too was asleep. The next time that she woke up they had both turned over, his arm was round her, warm and tight, and he was breathing in her ear, his head resting against hers. She knew by the sound of the breathing that he was deeply asleep, and she could allow herself the luxury of analysing her feelings. It was rather odd to discover, for a start, that it was extremely pleasant to be lying thus. The hard muscular body was completely relaxed, and although his arm was heavy, it was not uncomfortably so. Twelve hours previously she hadn't even known of his existence, she didn't even know his surname now, and yet here she was, comfortably half asleep in his arms—more or less—in extremely close proximity, to put it mildly, and feeling utterly and absolutely safe. It was a bizarre situation to say the least.

She made a mental apology to him. He had spoken the truth. He had been tired—and he had made no attempt at anything to which she could take exception. The night was not yet over, but she sensed that her feeling of security would not be shattered. And so, thinking those thoughts, she fell asleep again.

He woke her up with his movements, and she lay, eyes closed, wondering what he was doing. Then she realised. He was easing himself away from her. The next moment the blanket was tucked securely round her and she was alone in their makeshift bed. She heard him putting his shoes on, and kept her eyes closed until he went out of the room. She heard the back door open and close and snuggled down under the blankets. The room was intensely cold. Turning her head, she saw the dead ashes of the fire. She lay and waited for him to return.

He moved quietly, and she heard wood being broken and put in place, then a match flared, came a crackling, he muttered something under his breath, then: 'Ah!' It seemed time for her to awake officially. She sat up, rubbing the sleep from her eyes, and he added: 'Morning.'

'Good morning.'

'Did you sleep well?'

'The floor was a bit hard, but—yes, well enough, thanks.' Perhaps he was going to be civil. She certainly hoped so.

'So did I. You woke me up at one point, trying to grab the blankets.'

'I had none over me——'

'Right, don't let's fight. Save your energy for work.'

'Work?' she croaked. Visions of dusting and Hoovering and cooking flashed into her mind and were instantly dispelled, as he added:

'We're going outside to weigh up the situation, see what's what. Have you nothing to wear except those ridiculous shoes?' he nodded to her driving shoes, which were flat, and which Beth privately considered very sensible. But perhaps, on reflection, not for deep snow.

'I've a pair of rubber boots in the boot of my car, but I didn't think——'

'No, you wouldn't. I'll get them when we've had break-fast.' He turned away to feed the fire delicately with some thinner pieces of wood. 'Pour out two coffees, will you? It'll only be lukewarm now, and we'll have another sandwich each.'

Her stomach protested at the thought. Oh, for bacon and eggs and fried bread—she pushed that thought firmly away, and did as she was bid. The coffee was, as he said, only lukewarm, but it was certainly better than none. The sandwich only whetted her appetite for more and she looked hungrily at the two remaining in the paper.

'No,' he said.

'I wasn't going to——'

'Your look was enough.' He wrapped them up and put them to one side, and Beth scrambled to her feet.

'I'm going out to the back.'

'Don't be long. You can wear those to the car. It'll save time, and bring your rubber boots back.' He con-tinued feeding the now warm and lively fire, and she went out. When she returned he had his coat on too. 'Ready?' he said.

'Yes.' But she wasn't prepared for what greeted them as he opened the door. A white wall three feet high met them, and she gasped in dismay.

'It's not as bad as it looks,' he said, and walked into it. 'Close the door behind you—keep the heat in.' She obeyed, and followed, which was easier for her because he made a path through. The snow glittered in the morn-ing sun, and was beautiful. Slowly they went on, and there were no sounds, only the crunch of the snow as it was pushed aside. Nothing else was visible, either, save for tall trees. The hedge they had broken through was completely snow-covered, hiding the cars. He made his way towards it and found the gap, then Beth saw the abandoned cars, her blue, his red, only the top halves barely visible. Her heart sank. It seemed impossible to ever visualise them moving.

He reached her car and turned, and she saw the sweat on his brow. She also saw him properly for the first time. She knew his hair was black, but she had only seen his features in shadow before, never in daylight. He said something, but she was scarcely aware of it, for she was looking at him, not listening. He had a strong face, the face of a man who had lived, and seen the world, and held the traces of the mysteries in his dark grey eyes—and would survive whatever happened. The dark eyes and thick brows, the broad straight nose above a wide sensual mouth, the cleft in his chin, all added up to something overpoweringly attractive. He hadn't shaved, naturally enough, and this gave him a piratical appearance, and she felt herself shiver. Suppose he had tried to kiss her? She was immediately horrified at the thought. Whatever had put that idea into her head?

'Are you listening? I said—where are your keys?'

'Oh—sorry.' Flustered, she handed them to him and he opened the boot, with difficulty, for the lock was not only covered with snow, it was frozen. My God, she thought, he looks like a man who doesn't give a damn about anything. So why shouldn't he want me at Witchwood?

'Here,' he handed her the boots. 'Put them on now.'

'Yes.' She hopped and did as he said, because he liked instant obedience, and she was in no mood to defy him. He held the boot lid open.

'Anything else in there we can use?' he said, more to himself than to her. She didn't think so, but forbore to say it. He would probably decide the tow rope she always carried could be useful, and she wasn't going to argue about that either.

'No.' He slammed it shut and put her keys in his jacket pocket. 'I'll mind them.' He walked round to the front of her car and left her standing, waiting.

'I might have some chocolate in the car,' she shouted, remembering.

'Get it. Don't just stand there,' came the impatient reply. She put out her tongue at him and walked round to open the door. Bossy pig! she thought.

'What did you say?'

She felt herself go red. Had she muttered it out loud? 'Nothing. Just thinking.'

She struggled in and began to search frantically, stifling a giggle. It was really amazing what you could find that you had forgotten about, when you put your mind to it. She was glad she hadn't had time to thoroughly tidy out her car before setting off. In her glove compartment, behind the duster, was a bar of chocolate and a half empty bag of boiled sweets, a box of matches and three sticks of chewing gum. It was like a treasure trove.

He was at his own car now, brushing the snow off the top. 'Do the same to yours,' he shouted. 'They can be seen from the air more easily.'

It was eminently sensible. Beth only wished she had thought of it first. 'Right,' she answered, and set to.

Five minutes later they were standing outside his car and he held a small cardboard box he had brought from the boot. She looked at it, but didn't speak.

'Don't you want to know what's in here?' he asked.

She gave him a sweet smile. 'It's hardly polite to ask,

is it? I found the chocolate, and some matches, and sweets, and chewing gum.'

'Bully for you,' was the dry comment. 'Let's go back. We can have a meal—a proper meal now—isn't that nice?'

She thought for a moment he was being sarcastic about her find, but she found out when they reached the cottage what he meant. He slammed the door closed, and the fire greeted them, and Beth went over to the window and did something she had wanted to do ever since they arrived. She took out her duster and cleaned the window. The room was shades lighter immediately. She turned round, pleased, and he laughed. 'Typical woman,' he said mockingly. 'Why don't you clean the paintwork while you're at it?'

'There's no need to be sarcastic,' she retorted. 'It needed doing. At least we can see now.'

'How true.' He sat on the blanket. 'Come and see what I've got.'

He opened the cardboard box. It was full of food— tins of soup and meat apparently, from where she stood. She knelt down. 'Oh,' she exclaimed. 'Oh!' It was like Aladdin's cave of riches. She looked up, her eyes shining. 'How could you have forgotten that?'

'They're a present I had, that's all. But we've sufficient to last us a week now, and we'll certainly be out of here before that.' He picked one up. 'Go on, look at it.' She took the tin from him. The writing was foreign—what looked like Greek. The surprises were coming too thick and fast for her to take all this in.

'I've just come back from Greece,' he said, almost gently, for him. 'And I always take some with me to Witchwood, because Adam—the old man—your grand-father——' he paused, 'likes interesting new things from all over the world. But you'd already know that, wouldn't you?'

'No. I've never—met him.'

'I see.' He smiled and began to lift out the tins. The smile said it all. It said—I haven't even begun to question you, but it can wait.

'No, damn you,' she said sharply. 'You don't *see* at all!' She was astonished at her own outburst, but she couldn't stop now. 'So don't sit there smirking to yourself. I know what you're thinking——'

'You don't,' he cut in. 'You haven't the faintest idea. And don't raise your voice to me, it'll not get you any-where——'

'I'll shout if I like!' she retorted, eyes blazing. 'Try and stop me. You think you know it all. Well, you don't know anything about me for a start!'

'Precisely.' His voice effectively silenced her. 'But I intend to. Before we leave here, I intend to know all there is to know—and why you're going there pretending to be——'

Beth did something she had never intended to do. She lashed out and hit him hard. Then she jumped up and ran—only there was nowhere to run to, no way of escape, and by the window he caught her, grabbed hold of her, and pulled her to face him. 'You bitch,' he grated. 'You hot-tempered little bitch!'

'Let me go!' She was physically frightened of what he might do to her, but she faced him defiantly, willing him to release her. She must not admit her fear.

'You need a good spanking,' he said, then let her go abruptly. 'You'd just better be grateful I don't go around hitting women. A temper like yours needs curbing.'

'Then don't accuse me of lying!' she shot back. 'What would you do if someone said you were a liar?'

He looked at her for a moment, then the corner of his mouth twitched. 'Probably punch them on the jaw.'

'Right! That was the nearest I could get. If I were a man I would have done.'

'If you were a man,' he said slowly, 'you'd not still be on your feet after hitting me like that.' He turned away. 'But I wouldn't advise you to make a habit of it.'

'I won't—if you mind your words.'

He turned back. 'Don't tell me what to say or what not to say,' he answered swiftly. 'You're hardly in a position to give orders round here.' His eyes gleamed darkly. 'And don't make me lose my temper. I'm holding on to it very well, considering, but much more from you and I'll teach you a lesson you'll not forget in a hurry.'

'Are you threatening me?' She felt more confident now that the physical danger had passed—if indeed it had existed, which she doubted. She couldn't understand her own recklessness, yet something drove her on to defy him. She had never met a man like him before, and it was as if some spark of resentment prompted her to see how far she could go. It was almost as if she were an onlooker at the scene; horrified at herself, yet unable to control her tongue.

'Take it how you like,' he answered. 'You'll find out if you push me much further, won't you?'

'You're—you're insufferable!' she breathed. 'Pompous and arrogant—and I wish——'

'Don't stop there,' he said, after she had paused for breath. 'It's fascinating to hear your little insults. Are you stuck for words? How about "aggressive"? You've not said that yet, or "male chauvinist pig"——'

'Oh, get lost!' She whirled away and glared at the window. He laughed, then he held her so that she couldn't move, and he was right behind her, close, too close, and his voice came softly in her ear :

'Don't spoil that pretty face with temper. It doesn't become you.' She couldn't breathe. She was stifled, and now frightened in a much different way from before. Because many men had kissed her, but never one like this, and she had thought about it before, when she had looked at him properly for the first time and seen that virility and power, and been stirred by something she could not define, and she knew what he intended now, because she had an instinct about these things and had had to fight off many passes—and now she wasn't sure if she wanted to. Because she knew, suddenly, that she wanted very much for him to kiss her. He turned her round to face him, and she was only frightened of herself, not of him. He bent his face to hers, until his lips were a mere whisper away, then he laughed, very softly, and she saw his eyes, darker and deeper than any she had ever seen, saw what was in them gradually turn to amusement, as he said quietly : 'But I'm not going to— because I don't want to.' And he laughed again. Incensed, forgetting all his warnings, insulted and humiliated beyond words, she struck him hard across his face.

There was a shattering silence. Then he crushed her to him and kissed her with a force and savagery she had never known, his lips searching, seeking, his hands caressing her body.

Then it was over. He pushed her away. 'Satisfied?' he said harshly. 'It was what you wanted, wasn't it?'

Wordlessly she stared at him, tears of pain filling her eyes. Her skin felt raw from the scraping of his beard on her face. She felt cheap. He tilted her chin up slightly. 'Well, well,' he mocked. 'Not what you expected? Then don't play with fire or you'll get more than your fingers burned. You shouldn't give out the signals if you don't want what you're asking for.' He took his hand away from her face. 'Just remember what I said. We may have another night here together—don't forget that.' He turned away and went over to the fire, and it was as if she were dismissed.

Beth still trembled. No man had ever treated her so roughly. And there was not a thing she could do about it. He had effectively humiliated her—and she would never forget that as long as she lived.

'Are you coming over for some food or not?' he asked.
'No.'

'Suit yourself. I'm going to eat, when I can get one of these tins open. And we'll save the tins. They'll do to heat water in.' He began searching in his pockets, and she watched him find a penknife, watched the performance as he struggled to open one of the tins. She didn't doubt that he would do it. She hated him!

He began to whistle softly, prising open the tin as he did so. Then he sniffed, 'Ah, lovely!' The tin was crammed with sausages. He lifted one out and ate it slowly. 'Pity we've no forks. Still, never mind.'

Her stomach protested violently, and he looked at her. 'There's no point in standing on your dignity,' he remarked. 'Not here. It's too cold, and you need food to keep you alive, so come and sit down and eat.'

'You're a beast!'

'You've said that before—no, you haven't. That was one you'd not thought of. Perhaps I am—but you asked for all you got. Now come and eat. I won't tell you again.' She sat down on the floor and he handed her the tin. 'Five each,' he said. 'Then we melt some snow in the tin and make coffee.'

She began to eat. 'Coffee? How?'

'I've a small packet of ground coffee beans in the box.

Greek, quite strong, but you'll probably enjoy it. We have our flask cups to drink out of.'

It all seemed so organised, logical and simple. He could probably arrange a three-course meal from what he had, without any difficulty at all. She took three more sausages and handed him the tin. 'You can have the extra one,' she said. 'You're bigger than me—and you're doing more work.'

He shrugged. 'Okay. Do you like them?'

'They're delicious.' She gave a little sigh. 'I'm sorry I lost my temper.'

'It happens. We're not living under easy conditions. Eat up.' He finished his, the tin was empty and he stood up. 'I'll go and clean this out and pack it with snow. It should be an interesting experiment if nothing else.'

He vanished outside and she waited for him to return. For the moment it seemed that a truce existed. But for how long?

When he returned and pushed the tin into the flames and the snow started to melt, she said, 'I've got an idea,' and unscrewed the cups from the flasks. 'I'll fill these with snow and as that melts, we'll keep topping it up.'

'Clever girl.' He was too busy making sure the tin didn't overbalance to look at her, but he didn't sound as if he were being sarcastic. Beth went out, packed the cups with snow, and returned. The next fifteen minutes or so were busily occupied with scooping snow into the tin, adding the ground coffee, and watching to see what happened. At last the water began to bubble and it seemed a major success. Ryan held the lid with a handkerchief round his fingers and lifted the tin from the flames. 'Cups ready,' he said. 'Here we go,' and poured.

They sipped, they tasted, then they looked at one

another. It was drinkable, not the best Beth had ever drunk, but certainly passable black coffee.

'Mmm,' he said thoughtfully. 'Interesting.'

'True. And hot—ah! Why don't we add some from my flask?'

'Good thinking.' She did so, and they drank. There was an improvement immediately.

'I could get to like this,' he said. 'It's surprising what you can do with a little imagination.' Then he looked at her. 'And now,' he added, 'I think it's time we talked, don't you?'

It was the swift change of subject that caught her mentally off-balance—probably precisely what he intended. 'Surely we don't,' she said. 'My life is my business——'

'Except where it concerns someone I think a great deal about. Namely Adam Linden. And don't think you can come along out of the blue, announce you're his granddaughter and expect me to say "oh yes, fine" because I won't.' He finished his coffee and put the cup down. 'So you'd better tell me exactly who you are, and more important, why you're going there now, of all times. You may start talking.'

There was something he had said—now, of all times—and in the middle of her confusion that was even more puzzling, and somehow significant. She filed it away mentally. 'Look,' she said, 'it's quite simple. He—my grandfather, that is—had two sons, Adam and Norman. They both left home when young—perhaps after family quarrels, I've never managed to find out about that bit, and both eventually married. But they'd lost touch with their father by that time, and as far as I know, he wasn't aware of either marriage. Adam became very successful in business—Norman was an artist. Not as wealthy as his brother, but comfortable. They were always quite close, even though they mixed in different circles. Both of them were killed seven years ago in the Boeing air disaster in the Atlantic—you remember? My mother left home when I was young, and her sister brought me up. I'd heard her mention the old man, but never taken much notice because my father had always made him out to be a hard, ruthless old man—I even thought he was dead.'

She looked at him, and tears filled her eyes. 'A short time ago I heard that my mother, whom I'd not seen since I was a child, had died. My aunt had brought me up—but she did it out of a sense of duty, which she made clear to me, frequently. My father paid her well, and I saw him as often as I could, on his travels, but when he died she changed, became resentful. It might be because she had never married, I don't know, but I was made to feel—not wanted, I suppose. Two years ago I left her and rented a flat in London. My—dad— had left me well provided for. But don't you see—I had nobody——' she paused. 'Then I read something about Adam Linden in the paper, and wondered—the name isn't all that common. I made enquiries, checked up, and found that I had a grandfather. Two days ago I decided to go and find him, in person.' She stopped and closed her eyes. 'And that's my story. Satisfied?'

'Whose daughter are you? Adam or Norman?'

'Does it matter? Adam—the successful one.' She couldn't hide the note of bitterness in her voice. 'Don't you *believe* me?'

Ryan looked at her, his face cool and hard. 'Have you any proof?'

'My God! You don't!' she stood up in her agitation, and stared down at him. 'You *don't believe* me!'

'He's a very wealthy man.' He rose slowly to his feet. 'I didn't say I didn't believe you——'

'It's on your face!' she spat out. 'I can see it! What do you want? My birth certificate?'

'Keep cool. And *listen*. You've told me a very moving little story, but you have to admit it's all a little pat——'

'You think I've rehearsed it,' she stormed—she whirled away from him and crossed to the window, beating on the sill in her frustration. 'Why? Why?'

'Because now, of all times—it's odd you should suddenly decide——'

He'd said it again. 'What do you mean—now, of all times—why now? What's so special about *now*?'

'He recently had a heart operation. He's not a strong man, in fact, he's quite frail—and he's thinking of getting married to a very nice woman I admire and like very much. He's not had a happy life. He's finding some happiness now, for the first time in years—and I don't want to see it spoiled by anything—or anyone.' He paused to let the words sink in.

'You'd like me to go away? I've come too far for that. He's a blood relative, you're not. I only want to see him —can't you understand, or do you have a lump of steel where your heart should be? Do you?'

'You could upset him—disturb him—remind him of what's past and gone, if you went now, just like that.'

'You can't stop me,' she burst out. She was crying now, tears rolling down her face.

'No, I can't. I would if I could. I'm sorry—I know him and you don't. The shock could—kill him.'

She stared. 'You're over-dramatising the situation! You can't mean——'

'I can. To have someone step out of the past—a grand-daughter——'

'No. *No!*' she shook her head. 'Please—no.'

'I'm sorry, but it's the truth. He is frail, and he is old, and his last years should be peaceful—as they are now he's found Ruth.' He came over and gripped her arms. 'You're determined to go, aren't you?'

'Yes,' she whispered. 'I have no one—no relatives—please understand.'

He took a deep breath. 'There is one way you could go there—and stay there and be accepted, and not—upset him—but you might not like it. You could go with me—as my wife.'

CHAPTER THREE

BETH began to laugh hysterically at that. After all that had been said, to hear him say what he had—to expect her to—she couldn't stop, and she was frightened and gulping for breath—until he slapped her cheek. The shock brought her back to sanity. Wide-eyed, she stared at him, her breathing unsteady.

'I'm sorry,' he said. 'I had to stop you.'

'I know.' She sat down weakly, on the blanket. She was cold, and she shivered.

'I'll make you some more coffee. Better still, I'll warm what's left in my flask. It won't take a moment. You'll feel better when you've drunk it.' She waited, feeling numb. She watched him pour the coffee out and warm it in the tin, and when it was hot he poured something into it from a small bottle in the cardboard box, then handed it to her. 'Get that down you. I've put a drop of cognac in.'

'You think of everything, don't you?' She sipped, and felt better.

'Yes. And when *you've* thought about what I said you'll realise it's not such a mad idea after all. It will ease you into the household with no fuss, no excitement.'

She was already thinking about it. Looked at one way, it was so logical—but there was another aspect, several in fact. They weren't logical at all. She looked at him over the brimming cup, and he said softly: 'I know what you're thinking—but don't.'

'If they think we're married, they're going to give us

a bedroom—a shared bedroom, aren't they?'

'Naturally. But I'll make sure it's one with twin beds. I have no designs on you. We've already spent one night in much closer proximity than that and I didn't make a pass at you, did I?'

'No, but——'

'Listen. I travel all over the world—I'm an anthropologist. I study human and animal behaviour and living conditions in some of the remotest spots on earth, and I've lived alone for months at a time in extreme heat and extreme cold, and I've lived in native villages and with Eskimos—and I've survived. And I haven't gone crazy because there were no women——' he smiled quite gently. 'In other words, I shan't go mad with lust just because we're together, because I've trained myself to a fair pitch of self-control. You're far safer with me than you would be with any of your boy-friends, I can promise you.'

'But—but you *kissed* me!' she burst out.

'If I hadn't I'd have probably put you over my knee and walloped you! Good grief, woman, you were absolutely maddening!'

'All right—you made your point,' she said hastily. 'You promise—no strings?'

'No strings, I promise.'

'And then what?'

He shrugged. 'If—when he's used to you, accepting you—and he will—then we'll see. Let each day take care of itself. I'll think of something.'

And you can bet on that, Beth thought wryly. She finished the coffee, and she was calmer, and warmer, and his idea had sunk in to the extent that it no longer seemed bizarre. It seemed quite sensible. More—it seemed an ideal solution. And yet——

'Look,' she said, 'I know it may sound silly, but—well, I hardly know how to put it—only if we're—er—sharing a room, isn't it rather personal? Er—I mean——'

'You mean the little personal things, like getting undressed—and you putting your curlers in——'

'I don't! My hair's naturally curly,' she interrupted, 'but—the other—yes——'

'I know which room I'll insist on. It has a fabulous view, so he won't be surprised—and it has its own bathroom. No problems.'

'Why—why can't I just be your girl-friend, or even your secretary?'

'I've never had a secretary in my life. And as for your first question—quite logical. But——' he paused, 'Ruth has a nephew she's adopted.' Another pause. 'Now, I like Ruth, she's smashing, about sixty, full of fun. Her nephew is——' he paused again, 'how shall I put it delicately? A wolf. You won't have a minute's peace from him, unless you happen to be well and truly tied to me. So you see, I'm doing it for your sake as well.'

He had an answer to everything. She stared helplessly at him. Logic again. He didn't want the boat rocking with any trouble from Ruth's nephew—and she suspected it was not so much for her sake as for that of her grandfather and his bride-to-be.

'You must think an awful lot of my grandfather,' she said.

'I do. He's been like a father to me. I'm like you, I have no relatives, no family at all. I'll do anything to protect him—and this way, I can.'

'You don't like Ruth's nephew. What's his name?'

'No, you're right, I don't. I think he's a lazy devil personally—but I'm polite enough when we meet. I don't think he particularly likes me. His name is Ralph.'

'Hadn't you better tell me your surname? It would help to know my "married" name,' she said.

'My name is Ryan Drago. My grandfather came from Rumania. He and Adam Linden met before the first world war and remained friends until my grandfather died. So I'm a quarter Rumanian. Any more questions?'

'Yes. Where did we meet and marry?'

'We'd better plan something nice and simple. Whereabouts do you come from?'

'London.'

'I was there eight months ago, after I'd been up to Witchwood for a week. We met at a mutual friend's house, went out once or twice, and wrote after I left for Greece. I came back last week and we decided to get married on the spur of the moment, so we got a special licence and this is our honeymoon. Right?'

'It's so—I don't like lying,' she said desperately. 'I know—I understand the reasons—but I hate deceiving people.' She put her hand to her forehead—'I'm sorry, it sounds stupid, I know, but——'

'There is no choice,' he said gently. 'Believe me. His health is precarious.'

'But he's getting married——' she burst out. 'Surely——'

'For companionship, that's all. Ruth is already living at the house. She looks after him, and she loves him dearly. He's not had much love in his life. I don't know the rights and wrongs of why your father and his brother left—and I don't care, after all this time. Isn't it kinder to let him live his life out with what he has now?'

'Yes, you're right.'

'Then it's settled?'

She nodded. 'Yes, it's settled.'

*

She had time to think about her decision during the rest
of that long day. Ryan had brought some magazines
from his car, and notebooks, and while he wrote busily,
she read the magazines from cover to cover. It snowed
again, mid-morning, then stopped. Oh, for a radio, for
anything to relieve the boredom, she thought. It was as
though she were alone. Ryan, immersed in whatever he
was doing, might not have been there. He was in a world
of his own. He paused briefly to open a tin of soup at
lunchtime, asked her if she could manage to heat it, and
withdrew into his writing. It was while she was balancing the tin on the fire that she heard the sound of a
helicopter. She shouted something, she didn't know what,
stuck the tin on the hearth and dashed to the door,
followed by Ryan.

Hovering low over their cars was a police helicopter.
They ran towards it shouting and waving, slithering and
sliding through the snow—and saw an answering wave.
Then a loudspeaker boomed: 'Anyone needing urgent
help?' The voice echoed tinnily in the still air. Ryan
cupped his hands and shouted:

'We're okay. Enough food for several days.'

'Snowplough will try and clear tomorrow. They're
trying to get the major roads clear now. Everywhere's
in chaos. Just sit tight until it comes.'

Ryan gave the thumbs-up signal, the helicopter dipped
slightly, as if in salute, then whirred away, gaining
height rapidly and soon vanishing into the sullen sky. He
looked at Beth. 'Well, at least someone knows we're
here,' he said. 'And tomorrow——'

'Yes, I heard.' She gave a little smile. 'We're probably
a lot better off than some people. We'd better go and
get our soup.' They set off trudging back.

Much later, when it was dark and silent, and the fire

burned brightly in the hearth, and they had eaten their last meal of the day, Ryan said: 'We'll have an early night tonight. We don't know what time the snow-plough will be through in the morning and we're going to have to shift the cars out of the way when they get here.'

Beth hadn't thought of that. It seemed sensible—as everything he said did. 'Of course.' There had been a definite truce all day, and she preferred it to the aggression and fighting, which had exhausted her. She longed for a hot bath—even a good wash would do, but there was no water, only what they could melt of the snow, and nowhere to put that in any case. She compromised by cleaning her face and hands with cleansing cream and wiping it off with tissues. Seeing him watching her, she held the jar out. 'Want some?'

'No. I'm used to being dirty.' He grinned. 'Perhaps I could have phrased that better—I've often been in places where it was impossible to wash for days. There's always the snow anyway. I can go and rub my face in that before I go to sleep.' He rubbed his stubbly face. 'I should have a shave, though—only trouble is, my razor's in the car and I can't be bothered.'

He looked so different when he grinned. He looked quite human. Beth surprised herself. 'I'll go and get it,' she offered. 'I've done nothing all day and the exercise will do me good.'

He looked at her. 'You mean it?'

'Yes. Where is it?'

'Glove compartment, battery electric—saves time when I'm driving.'

'You don't——'

'Shave as I go along? Yes, if I'm in a hurry. The car's not locked.' Beth put on her coat and boots and opened the door to an icy blast of snow-flurried wind. For a moment she almost regretted her impulsive offer, then, taking a deep breath, she set off.

It was strange to be completely alone in the eerie half light of the snow where nothing moved, and the world was a cold lonely place, yet with a beauty all of its own. Beth walked carefully and slowly towards the hedge, and wondered how she would have managed had she been entirely on her own. She looked up at the sky, and snowflakes brushed her face and hair, and a wind gently sighed around her and she felt suddenly very sad.

She reached Ryan's car and, opening the door, sat in the driving seat, switched on the interior light and opened the glove compartment. There was the usual clutter of cleaning cloths, de-icer aerosol spray, folded up maps. She lifted them out carefully and pushed her hand to the back and found the razor. A flat wallet fell out on to the floor, and as she bent to pick it up, it opened. Only it wasn't a wallet, it was a leather photo holder, and it contained two photographs. She couldn't have closed it without looking even if she had wanted to—and she didn't want to.

One photograph was of Ryan with a woman, the other of him, the woman, and a young boy. They looked happy —they looked a family. Beth was shaken, although she could not have said why. She looked more closely at the photograph, especially at Ryan's face. He was younger, and the photograph could have been taken five or six years previously. He had been married—or he still was. Yet what had he said? That he was alone in the world? There was something disturbing about the photographs, and she didn't know what it was. She closed the folder and replaced it firmly at the very back of the glove compartment, put in the duster and oddments, and slid out of the car. It didn't matter; it was nothing to do with her at all, she knew.

She set off to return to the house, but the memory of the faces she had seen lingered until long after she had gone to bed, and she lay unmoving on her side, watching the dying shadows of the fire dancing on the walls, and hearing the breathing of the sleeping man whose body kept her warm and safe.

Ryan had gone when she woke the next morning, but a small fire was alight, and a tin of water sizzled gently, balancing cleverly on another empty tin, and she knew that he wasn't far away.

Then she heard the noise from outside and went to the door. Over the hedges she glimpsed the giant rumbling snowplough, and heard men shouting. A strange sense of mingled relief and dismay filled her. Now they could leave. Their imprisonment was over—but something else was just beginning. For the first time she felt apprehensive about what she was going to do. It had all seemed so simple before—but Ryan had changed all that.

Beth looked round the room and began to gather together all her possessions, ready to pack. She folded the blankets and put them together with Ryan's notebook and magazines in the corner. When he returned shortly afterwards she had made the coffee and eaten her half of the tin of spiced herrings he had left open. He looked across from the door at her. 'We can get through later,' he said, 'in about an hour, when the plough has finished clearing the road ahead. We should be at Witchwood in three hours.'

Three hours. Not long in which to become a different

person, to assume a new role. 'Yes. What about my car? It'll look odd if we arrive separately, won't it?'

'We pass a town in about eight miles. There's a garage you can leave it at. We'll load all your stuff in mine when we set off, and I'll take you there.'

'I don't have a wedding ring,' she said, and the words, for some reason, didn't come easily.

He shrugged. 'So what? People don't bother these days.'

'But——'

'If it bothers *you*, we'll see if there's a jeweller's in the town. No problem.'

She turned away without a word and began to pack the extra sweaters in her case, together with her make-up bag. She had made up as best she could, with only the window for a mirror, and she longed for a bath.

'Are you having doubts?' Ryan was drinking his coffee, watching her.

'Of course I'm having doubts,' she snapped. 'You make it so—so cold-blooded, somehow.'

He gave her a brief laugh. 'Perhaps I'm a cold-blooded person. I've told you, it's the only way.'

'So you say! You might be lying, for reasons of your own.'

There was a brief silence. Tension filled the room. 'Then you'll see for yourself if I am when we reach there, won't you?' he said softly, and his words sent a cold trickle down her spine. He was hard, and he was ruthless, she knew that. She wondered if he ever thought about the woman in the photograph—and where she was now. There was no way she would ever ask.

'We'll be there in fifteen minutes,' Ryan said. Beth looked out at the distant hills and the trees. Everywhere was snow-covered and beautiful. She touched the new wedding ring on her finger. It was like wearing a brand.

They had left the cottage much as they found it. He had extinguished the fire with snow, put the empty tins in the tattered dustbin outside the back door and taken a last look around while Beth waited. Then they had gone out, closing the door behind them, made their way to the cars, and packed everything in the back of his. The snowplough had cleared a way of sorts, and the road to Witchwood stretched ahead, and soon she would be there. She negotiated her car almost into a ditch, and he passed her and waited until she had started up, then drove off. They soon reached the town, where she rented a garage at the back of the petrol station and went into Ryan's car. Then he found a jeweller's shop and stopped outside it. 'Shall I get it, or you?' he asked, much as though he were wondering who should buy the groceries.

'I will.' She slammed the door and went into the shop and bought the most reasonably priced ring she saw. It was a plain simple gold band that fitted her perfectly.

Then they were off on the last stage of their journey. It was nearly lunchtime, she remembered thinking that as they neared a petrol station in the middle of countryside, with a café at the side. 'Can we stop for a coffee?' she asked.

Ryan gave her a sidelong glance. 'If you wish,' and he drove on the forecourt, then parked at the side. The chatty woman who served them was full of the snowstorm, and told him that they were the first customers for three days.

'Been stuck in the snow, have you?' she beamed over the counter at Beth, who sat at a red-topped table wondering if the coffee would dispel the butterflies in her stomach.

'Yes, we stayed at an empty cottage about fifteen miles back,' she answered.

'Fancy that! You were lucky. I heard on the radio that they've rescued dozens of people stranded in cars. Some of them near freezing, they were. Real nasty weather, it was.' She sniffed and looked at Ryan who was putting sugar in his coffee. 'You and your husband going far?'

You and your husband. The words were like a hammer blow. 'No, not far now,' Ryan answered for Beth. 'We're going to stay at Witchwood. But my wife fancied a coffee before we reached there, so here we are.' He smiled pleasantly at the woman.

'Ah, that's right, Witchwood. Beautiful place. They'll have been well and truly snowed up, being remote as they are, but I know Mrs Hoskins that cleans there, and she says they keep enough food in to withstand a siege!' she laughed. 'Well now, this won't get my work done, will it?' She waved aside Ryan's offer of the money for the coffee. 'On the house, my dear, you being stuck in the snow. Pity you hadn't reached here before it started. We've a spare bedroom—you'd have been comfier than your cottage!' and with that she bustled away to the kitchen.

Ryan called his thanks and carried the coffee to the table. 'Cigarette?' he produced his battered packet and opened it.

'No, thanks. You didn't smoke any more, did you?'

'No. I didn't know how long we'd be there, did I? I don't smoke many.' He lit one and put the packet away. Then he looked at Beth. 'What are you thinking?'

'I couldn't begin to tell you.'

'Well, I suggest you try and look more cheerful before we reach the house. You're on honeymoon, not going to a funeral.'

'Don't worry,' she answered quietly. 'I won't give the game away. Is that what worries you? We've made the bargain. I'll keep my part.'

He nodded. 'Drink up and we'll be on our way.'

'You haven't told me how long you—we—plan to stay.'

'Haven't I? There's no fixed time. Why? Do you have a job to get back to?'

'No. I do work, but for an office bureau, so I pick my own times.'

'And what do you do?'

'Do you really want to know?' she responded bitterly.

'I wouldn't be asking if I didn't.'

'The usual. Shorthand, typing, reception work.'

'Hmm, so you could do secretarial work for me if necessary?'

'I already told you that, and you said you'd never had a secretary——'

'I know. True. But I'm preparing a résumé of my last two years' work for the *National Geographical Magazine* —that's what I was writing at the cottage.'

'So?'

'So—if you're short of anything to do, you can do some typing for me. I'll pay you.'

'How kind,' she murmured, not troubling to hide the sarcasm.

He narrowed his eyes. 'Watch that tongue of yours. Try to remember who you are.'

'I'm your wife. I can't forget that, can I?' she retorted.

'For the time being, that's all.'

'Thank God!'

Ryan finished his coffee. 'We'd better go before we start a full-scale fight.' He took the empty cups to the counter. 'Thanks very much. We're off now.'

'Goodbye, safe journey.' The voice floated back from
the kitchen. They went outside into watery sunshine. It
made the banked-up snow glitter icily. Beth's mood was
precarious, balanced between anger and tears, and it was
as if he knew, for he drove only a short while down the
road before pulling to one side, stopping the car, and
turning to her.

'You need a good shaking,' he snapped. 'I've told you
why——'

'I know why. It doesn't make it any easier, does it?'
She glared at him, her eyes glistening with tears. 'I'll be
cheerful and pleasant. I'll be the perfect "wife", don't
worry. Now, is the lecture over or are we going to sit
here all day?'

He banged his fist down hard on the steering wheel.
'You are the most exasperating woman I have ever——'

'Shut up!' she shouted. 'Just shut up and leave me——'

He caught hold of her and his hands dug into her arms.
She saw the strain in his face, the dark anger in his eyes,
and was stilled by the force of it.

'Please,' she whispered. 'Let me go, you're hurting
me——'

He released her instantly as if the touch of her burned
him. 'You make me want to hurt you,' he said harshly.

She rubbed her arm where his fingers had been. Tension, like an electric current, filled the car. The air almost
tingled with it, and she could hardly breathe. 'I wish I'd
never come,' she said shakily.

'So do I. But you have.' He started the car again. 'Pull
yourself together—we'll be there very soon.'

Beth took out her lipstick, pulled down the sun-visor
and looked into the mirror to see her white face staring
back at her. No man had ever had the power that this
one had to reduce her self-control to shreds. Her fingers

were trembling as she applied the lipstick.

Then he was turning off the road and slowing down, and she looked in alarm. Not another lecture, she thought. Then she realised why. They had driven through a gateway and were in a drive, and it was impassable with the snow, only a thin trail cleared ahead of them. 'This is it,' he said, 'and it looks as if we'll have to walk to the house from here.' He got out and slammed his door, and Beth, after a momentary hesitation, followed suit. The tall trees that surrounded them effectively hid the house from view. Ryan turned to her. 'Leave everything here,' he said. 'I'll come down later, once I've taken you in,' and he began to walk along the narrow cleared track, wide enough for one person. Beth followed. The path curved, and the trees no longer hid the house. She saw it for the first time, in the distance, and she stood still, just looking, no longer caring about Ryan or anyone else in her reaction to her first sight of her grandfather's home.

CHAPTER FOUR

It was a tall, beautiful old house of granite, and the walls were smothered in ivy. It had a gracious welcoming air, and, surrounded by snow as it was, became almost a fairytale castle in appearance. Smoke rose from one of the many chimneys, and the windows caught the reflection of the sun, and shone. Beth held her breath for a moment. It was larger than she had visualised, certainly more beautiful—and she hadn't known anything about it until recently.

Ryan stopped, waited, and she caught up with him. 'I was only looking,' she said defensively.

'I know. That's how it gets you the first time. You want to see it inside as well.' Her heart ached in sudden pain. This was where her father had spent his childhood— yet he had never spoken about it. It was as if he had put it out of his mind, and she had never known why.

Ryan turned and walked on, and Beth followed. A small area of drive had been cleared at the front, as had the ten steps leading up to a wide front entrance. Tall imposing pillars stood either side of the porch, and two stone lions guarded it. Ryan pressed the bell, and the distant echoes came faintly back. Then they waited. He looked at her and she took a deep breath, then gave a shaky smile. 'See?' she said.

He turned away without a word as footsteps could be heard, then the door was flung open, and a grey-haired, middle-aged woman stood there.

'Ryan!' The delight on her face was obvious as she

stepped forward to greet him, and was enfolded in a bear hug.

'Ruth, it's good to see you again. We made it at last.' Still holding her, he turned, and looked at Beth. 'Ruth, this is Beth—my wife.'

Ruth's eyes widened, then she began to laugh. 'This is wonderful! Beth my dear, how lovely,' and she stepped forward and hugged the bemused Beth. 'You're a dark horse, Ryan,' she said, turning towards him. 'You arrive out of the blue like this and calmly introduce your wife! Well, well, come on in, the pair of you, and we'll get out of this cold.' She closed the door. They were in the wide hall with oak-panelled walls. A fire burned in a large fireplace, and shields hung on the walls, and a grand-father clock ticked solemnly away in a corner. Ruth flung open a door and they went into a large drawing room where another fire burned, and all was bright and cheerful, and there were two brocade-covered settees, one either side of the fireplace. 'Sit down and we'll have a drink,' said Ruth. 'Adam is resting, of course. We hadn't a clue when you'd arrive. The whole country's been at a standstill for two days, how on earth did you manage to get through?'

Ryan began to answer, and Beth only half listened, her eyes wandering round the room, taking it all in, feel-ing the warmth—the real warmth of a good fire, begin-ning to drive out the cold of the previous two days. She had liked the woman—her grandmother-to-be—instantly. It only made the deception seem shabbier, but she put that thought out of her head. It was too late now, she was committed.

'Sherry, Beth?'

'Please.'

'You must be starving. I'll get you something to eat

when you've drunk that. Oh, dear, how awful, having to sleep on the floor in an old cottage—and you on your honeymoon too!' Beth nearly choked on her sherry.

'We managed,' answered Ryan, in dry tones. 'Look, Ruth, I think Beth would like a bath before she eats— wouldn't you, love?'

The endearment sounded natural. 'I'd love one,' she answered.

'I don't suppose,' said Ryan winningly, 'that we could have the room with its own bathroom? The views are quite something. Beth would love that.'

'Well, of *course*,' agreed Ruth—'but it has twin beds——' she looked in comical dismay at them both. 'You don't——'

Beth wanted to curl up and die. She should have known that Ryan wouldn't be lost for an answer. He hadn't been up until now. He laughed. 'Ruth, love,' he said, 'it's more fun.' He emptied his glass and stood up. 'I'll go and get our cases,' he said. 'We've had to leave the car at the end of the drive, but I wanted to bring Beth in out of the cold first.'

'Of course you did. Poor girl!' Ruth gave her a sympathetic smile. 'I'll take you up. While you're having your bath I'll get your lunch ready. Come on, dear.'

Beth followed her up the wide staircase, along a wide corridor to a room at the end. 'It's away from the rest of the house,' said Ruth, going in and switching on an electric fire. 'So you can make as much noise as you like.' She looked at Beth in a motherly way. 'You're really very pretty,' she said. 'I'm so happy that Ryan's married again. I hope you'll be very happy.' She turned away and busied herself smoothing down the white lace bedspreads. 'There, that's tidy," she pronounced, as if the room had been a mess before. 'Here's your bathroom, dear,' she opened a mirror covered door to reveal a neat pink-tiled bathroom. 'Lots of hot water for you. While you're running it I'll go and get some towels.' She smiled and left Beth on her own. Beth walked to the window and looked out. The view was indeed magnificent, the rolling Derbyshire hills, snow-covered, stretching away into the distance, and a great sense of calm filled her. She was here, that was all that mattered. Ryan's behaviour couldn't be faulted—so far—and Ruth was a genuinely warm-hearted woman.

She went in and began to fill the bath. Minutes later she was soaking in the hot scented water, lying back while the aches and stiffness from floor sleeping were melted away. 'Ah!' she gave a deep blissful sigh. Never had a bath been more welcome—or more perfect. She began to soap herself lazily, taking her time.

A tap on the bathroom door made her jump. Ruth had already brought the towels.... 'Yes?' she called.

'It's me—Ryan.'

'I'm in the bath——' she began. The door wasn't locked. She watched the door handle in faint horror.

'I know. I have no intention of coming in, so relax. I've brought you your case. It's here, just outside the bathroom door—and don't worry, I'm going down now. I'll have a bath later.' She heard his footsteps recede, and relaxed again. For one moment she had thought he was going to come in. The pleasure was gone; he had shattered the calm. Beth finished soaping herself and stepped out on to the fluffy white rug. She dried and dressed herself, then went down to try and find the drawing room.

She met her grandfather for the first time when it was growing dark, and had started to snow again, and they were sitting in the drawing room drinking coffee. The fire burnt brightly, the lights were on, reflecting in the darkened windows, and she sat on the settee next to Ryan, listening to Ruth putting him up to date on all the local gossip. She was gently amusing, never malicious, as she told him of the doings of nearby villagers, and he would ask after someone, and she would go off on another track, and it was pleasant to just sit there, hearing it all.

Then a bell rang, and Ruth jumped. 'That'll be Adam,' she said.

'I'll go.' Ryan stood up. 'You stay and talk to each other.' He was gone.

Ruth smiled at Beth. 'He'll be down in a minute,' she said. 'I dare say Ryan will be telling him all about you. Did he tell you about Adam?'

Beth had to clear her throat. 'He—said he'd not been very well,' she answered.

'No. He's not in good health at all—but he's getting better. He's got a bad heart, and must rest. No excitement at all. That's why it's nice for Ryan to go and fetch him, he'll be able to break it gently about you.' She laughed. 'Heavens, that sounds bad!'

'I know what you mean.' Beth smiled. So Ryan had spoken the truth in that matter. 'And I'll be very quiet, I promise you.'

'Oh, no, he likes to talk, and laugh. Don't think we all go around with long faces, because we don't. But sudden excitement could bring on an attack. No, you'll do him good, my dear. He likes young people, and he thinks of Ryan as a son, of course. So by all means make a fuss, and talk as much as you like—ah, I hear them coming now.' She went over to open the door. Beth's heart pounded so loudly she thought everyone must hear it.

She turned her head slowly, then rose to her feet as Ryan came in the room, his arm under the elbow of the man beside him, gently and casually helping him. And Beth saw him for the first time, saw the kindly-faced, tall lean man with silver hair and a smile on his lips, and she felt a surge of a powerful emotion—and love. She wanted to cry out, to tell them—but she made not a sound. Then he came over to her and held out his hand.

'Beth—I hope I may call you that. This is truly a pleasure, my dear. Is an old man permitted to kiss the bride?'

'Of course.' She leaned forward and touched his cheek with her lips, and she was filled with the tears she dared not shed.

'Well, well, Ryan, you've made my day with the news. Ruth, my dear, I'll sit over there and then I can see you and Beth, and Ryan can sit beside me, and I'll have a coffee.'

'You won't,' retorted Ruth firmly. 'You remember what the doctor——'

'Pish to doctors!' Adam Linden snorted. 'Just a very weak one, eh?' he winked at Beth, who winked back.

'Mmm, well, very weak then,' Ruth agreed. 'More for you, Beth?'

'No, thanks. I'll sit and talk to Mr Linden if I may?'

'Don't call me Mr Linden—makes me feel old.'

'What would you like me to call you?'

'Call me Adam. Everyone else does.'

It seemed strange to be calling her grandfather by his christian name, but short of saying so, there was nothing Beth could do about it. 'Thank you, I will.'

The old man was seated comfortably by the fire with his feet up on a pouffe, and they began talking while they waited for Ruth to return. Ryan did nearly all the talking, and Beth was thankful. She was caught up in a situation she didn't feel able to cope with yet, and gathered her strength for the questions that would inevitably come. She wasn't prepared for her own reaction, to start with. The surge of affection had surprised her with its strength. Now, at last, she knew why Ryan had reacted as he had to her announcement at the cottage that she was Beth Linden, Adam's granddaughter. For she could understand the love he had for the old man—and his desire to protect him. The plan she had at first thought so outrageous no longer seemed so.

Gradually she grew calmer, and was able to join in the conversation easily, and she saw Ryan's eyes on her once, as she spoke, telling Adam of her work in London, and it seemed that he watched her coolly, shrewdly, as if he guessed her thoughts. Once he smiled at her, and all the aggression had gone. He had become a different man, gentle, courteous, amusing. She watched him unobserved, as he showed the old man some photographs of Greece. She watched him, seeing the great strength in his features, the hard line of his jaw softened in the firelight, his hands, the large hands, now gentle, as he handed the photographs over, and knew that here was a man of an immense depth of character, a man who would stand alone, and never falter in what he chose to do. She knew that what he had told her was true, at the cottage. She would be safe with him, no matter how many nights they spent together, or under what conditions. Because he had given his word.

He looked up, as if sensing her regard, and his eyes on her were dark and unreadable. And it was Beth who looked away first, lest he read what was in her mind. She felt vulnerable, and she felt confused. She had never met anyone like Ryan before. Every man she had met had tried, by fair means or foul, to get her into bed, until she wearied of the battle, and became distrustful, so that relationships were coloured by it, and she waited for the inevitable pass. Ryan had kissed her, but it had been more in anger than lust. She felt a vague stirring of some emotion she could not define, and it was a relief when Ruth came into the room again, interrupting her train of thought. The conversation eddied and flowed, and all was calm again, and Beth began to enjoy herself. The plans were made for the evening. Adam went up to bed at nine, and watched television in his room for a while. Dinner would be at eight, and Adam made it clear to Ryan and Beth that his house was theirs, and they were to do exactly as they pleased, within the limitations imposed by the weather. 'It's so nice to have you both here,' he said. 'Isn't it, Ruth?'

'It is indeed. But you're not to go dashing about, just because they're here,' she said. He sighed.

'See how she bosses me about?' he complained to Beth, but the warmth was there in his voice and in his eyes when he looked at Ruth, and Beth knew how deep his love for her was.

She smiled. 'I don't think you'd let anyone tell you what to do,' she answered. Ruth hooted with laughter.

'That's it, you tell him!'

'Ah, you women—you always stick together, eh, Ryan? You'll have to watch Beth doesn't start bossing you around. Put your foot down now, start as you mean to go on, that's what I say.'

'Precisely.' Ryan looked across at Beth, then he smiled. She knew it was solely for the others' benefit, but it didn't stop her heart bumping. 'When are you and Ruth getting married?'

'In three weeks. We planned it for when you're here. It'll be a very quiet ceremony, in the chapel, of course.'

'I shall look forward to it,' Ryan said gently.

'And you'll be best man?'

'I'll be honoured.'

'That's settled, then.' Adam looked across at Ruth. 'And I dare say Beth can be matron of honour, eh, if you ask her nicely?'

'What a lovely idea! Will you, Beth?'

'Yes, of course.' A sudden lump came into her throat, making it ache. Nothing like this had ever happened to her before. It was as if they were making her part of the family. She fought desperately for self-control, then Ryan asked Adam some question, and the attention was diverted from her, and she knew suddenly that he had done it deliberately, because he had seen.

Later, as she unpacked her clothes in the bedroom, she remembered the scene in the drawing room, and the ache came back at the memory. She left her case and went over to the window to cool her aching head on the glass. Her throat was raw with the unshed tears she had repressed before, and now they came freely. She didn't hear the door open, nor close again, and until Ryan's voice spoke from just behind her she was not aware that he was in the room. She jerked round as he said: 'What's the matter?' then she heard his sharply indrawn breath. She couldn't see him because she was blinded by the tears.

'Nothing.' Her voice was a croak. 'Nothing.' She turned away, shoulders shaking. 'Go away!'

'Not and leave you like that.'

She wanted desperately for him to take her in his arms

and comfort her, and the thought was as frightening as
her emotion. 'You wouldn't understand,' she said, sniff-
ing. Her body ached.

'Wait a minute. Here.' He pressed a handkerchief into
her hand. 'Dry your eyes.' She did so. 'You're here, aren't
you? It's what you wanted.'

He didn't understand. Nobody could. 'Yes, I'm here
—as your wife. I didn't l-let you d-down, did I?'

'You did it beautifully. They both like you.'

'Thanks!' she said bitterly, and turned away. Then
it happened. She felt his arms go round her, felt the
warmth and hardness of his body, and he turned her
gently to face him, and held her against him so that her
face was buried against his chest. For a few moments
he held her there silently, and she was filled with his
strength and a kind of heady warmth that enveloped her,
and she knew this was the only place she wanted to be,
and she knew, too, why.

He murmured something she couldn't hear properly,
and she looked up. His face was misty through the veil
of her tears. 'What?' she whispered.

'It doesn't matter. Are you better now?'

She took a deep, shaky breath. 'Yes. Let me—let me
go——'

'In a minute.' He bent his head, and there was only
the sweetness of him, and the feel of his mouth upon
hers, and she had never wanted anything else in her
life but this moment. Then it was over, and he stood
away and said softly: 'That was to replace the other
one—I'm not always brutal.' He turned and went out,
and left her alone.

It had cured the tears. Perhaps that was, after all, what
he had intended. Beth felt drunk, but she had not touched
alcohol since they first arrived. She felt light, and tingling,

and she touched her face and wondered at the absurdity of life, and why she should feel as she did. She knew she was falling in love with Ryan Drago, who was the last man she should ever have wanted. He was a loner, a man who travelled, and lived in a different world from hers—a man who didn't even like her. She stood very still as she realised that. If he was being nice, it would only be for one reason. She had been mistaken before, when she had looked at him and seen another side of him. He was like all the rest, no better. Perhaps more subtle, and certainly cleverer in his approach, but seeking only one thing. She had known, ever since she was old enough to be told by her aunt, that men were all the same. And she had found out for herself in the past four years the truth of that.

She sighed. Here we go again, she thought. Only this time I've got to watch myself, because with this one I might find myself in a situation I don't want to control. There was a silk-covered screen in one corner of the bedroom. She carried it over and put it out between the two beds, then smiled. It was hardly a fortress, but it afforded some privacy. She folded it up again and put it back, in case Ruth might come in for anything, although it seemed unlikely. Then she finished unpacking and went into the bathroom to wash. When Ryan came in again, she was in the bed by the window, the screen was in place, and she was reading a book. She couldn't see him, only hear him, then the short laugh, then:

'And what's this in aid of?' The next minute the screen was lifted and folded, and he stood there looking down at her.

'Leave it there!' she said angrily.

'No. Ruth may bring us in a cup of tea in the morning. She'd wonder, wouldn't she?'

'I don't care!'

'Don't be stupid. You've gone this far. We don't rock
the boat at this stage.' He put the screen back in the
corner. Beth looked helplessly on. 'Carry on with your
reading. I'm going to get a wash, then I'm going to sleep
—I'm tired.' He nodded, picked up his pyjamas from
the bed, and went into the bathroom. The door closed
firmly and then she heard water running. She felt rest-
less and knew she wouldn't sleep. This would be their
third night together. And how many more? It was no
use. She didn't even know what the book was about;
nothing had registered since she had first opened it. She
put it down and lay back, wide-eyed, staring at the ceiling. What was going on in Ryan's mind? He would bide
his time. He would be a man of infinite patience. And
what had he said about Ruth's nephew? That he was a
wolf. At least, thought Beth, I'd know where I stand
with *him*.

She heard the bathroom door open, and turned on her
side and closed her eyes. 'Are you going to sleep?' he
asked.

'Yes.' She didn't open her eyes. 'I thought you said
Ruth's nephew lived here.'

'He's away. He's due back any time—when he can
get through. Why, are you looking forward to meeting
him?'

'His aunt's very nice.'

'That doesn't answer my question. Of course she's
very nice—and he can be exceedingly charming, as I'm
sure you'll discover.'

'That'll be a change,' she murmured.

He gave a short laugh. 'And I'm not? Forgive me—
living in the wilds, as I so often do, I don't get time to
cultivate the social graces. However, don't forget you're

here as my wife. You'll be safe from his advances, which should set your mind at rest.' She heard him getting into bed, and judged it safe to turn round and look at him.

'It should, but it reminds me of a quote: *"Sed quis custodiet ipsos custodes?"*'

'My, but you're a Latin scholar as well, are you? "But who is to guard the guards themselves?" Did you think I wouldn't know it? Who is to protect you from *me*? Why, I've already told you. Me.' He smiled and turned out the light, leaving the room in darkness.

Quietly seething, Beth lay and saw the grey shadowy shape settle down for sleep. Ryan had an answer for everything, and he had effectively made her feel foolish and childish in just a few sentences. He was completely maddening! She heard a telephone ringing faintly from somewhere in the house, then it stopped. She wondered who it might be. It certainly wouldn't be for her, because nobody knew she was coming, which was just as well, considering the circumstances. It could be exceedingly embarrassing to have to explain away the surname Linden when she was supposed to be Mrs Drago. She said the last name softly inside her head. A strange name —a strange man. And on that thought, she fell asleep.

She dreamed about her grandfather, beautiful dreams of being welcomed in the house, and of him saying he had waited for her arrival for so long, and she must stay, because she was part of the family.... It must have been the last dream of the night, because a tapping on the door awoke her from it, and blended with the dream before she realised it was real.

'Hello?' she called. No answer. She slipped out of bed and went to the door and opened it. Outside on the floor was a tray with two cups of tea and a plate of biscuits.

She peeped out to see Ruth's figure vanishing round the corner. Dear Ruth, kind and tactful. Beth looked at the sleeping man lying on his side, sprawled across the bed, and thought, Oh God, if only she knew the truth. Perhaps, soon, she would.... It was no more than an intangible thought at the moment, and she put it aside as she picked up the tray, carried it in and set it down on a table. She put on her dressing gown before waking Ryan.

'Ruth's brought us tea,' she said crisply, because now it was morning, the silly fancies of the night had vanished, and she would never again let him see her vulnerable—lest he guess the truth....

'Hmm? What's the time?'

'Eight-thirty, and it's Sunday—I think.'

He sat up. 'Is it? Thanks.' This as she handed him the tray, after removing her cup and saucer.

'What time is breakfast?' she asked him.

'About nine usually.' He rubbed his face and yawned. 'I'm going to get my car moved today. Want to help?'

'Why not? How?'

'They've a small tractor here. It'll get through the snow and shift it. Then I'll drive the car up to the garage. It can't stay there, Ralph could be home any time.'

'And it wouldn't be fair if he couldn't get in.' Beth said it softly, and moved away as she spoke, and smiled to herself.

'Well, he sure as hell won't move the snow,' Ryan answered swiftly. 'Dear Ralph doesn't enjoy manual work.'

'And you do? Dear me, you don't like him, do you?'

'No.' He finished his tea. 'I'm going to have a bath, so if you want to use the bathroom, I suggest you do it now.'

Without another word she left him, went into the bathroom, and locked the door with a resounding click. She washed, realised she had left her clothes in the bedroom, and went out again. 'It's all yours,' she said.

'Thanks.' Ryan walked across the room, gathering clothes as he went. Then the door was bolted firmly after him, and she heard the water running into the bath. She gave him a few minutes to get into it, then quickly dressed. After doing so, she debated whether to go down or wait for him. A point of etiquette was involved. Did honeymooners have to go down to breakfast together? She decided that, quite frankly, she didn't care, shouted out through the closed door: 'I'm going down,' and went, taking the tray.

She found the kitchen after a brief search, tapped on the door and popped her head round. 'May I come in?'

'Of course, dear.' Ruth was busy at the cooker.

'Thanks. Ryan's having a bath and he'll probably take ages, so I thought I'd come down and see if I could do anything to help.' Beth looked round her appreciatively. The kitchen was large but had been modernised without losing its character, and a fire burned in the large fireplace with its old-fashioned oven beside it. Ruth saw Beth's glance on it and laughed.

'That old kitchen range was left in when Adam did up the kitchen. It's jolly useful in power cuts, I can tell you. I can put a casserole in there and it does beautifully.'

'I'm sure it does.'

'I don't need any help, thanks. Sit yourself down and have another cup of tea while you wait. Adam doesn't get up till about ten, so there's just the three of us. We'll eat out here where it's nice and warm.'

'We're going to clear the snow from the drive later,' Beth told her.

'Bless you! That'll be a good job done. I must say this about Ryan, he enjoys getting jobs done when he's here.' Ruth laughed. 'Still, you'll find out all about that as time goes on. Will you be travelling with him all over the world?'

Beth hadn't thought of that. She desperately wanted to tell Ruth the truth, but now was not the time. Not yet. 'Well, I suppose so,' she said. Perhaps it hadn't been such a good idea to go down alone. At least he always had answers ready. She felt wretched when telling lies, whereas it clearly didn't bother him. 'We'll discuss it while we're here.' She managed a bright smile at the older woman. 'There's the wedding to look forward to as well.'

'Aye, there is. It's a shame Adam has no blood relatives to be here——' Oh, but he will have, thought Beth, anguished, and if only I could tell!—'but it has to be very quiet anyway, so perhaps it's as well.'

'I'm looking forward to it,' she said, with truth. 'Did you mention it would be in a chapel?'

'Yes. In the grounds. You must get Ryan to show you. It's not far from the house——' At that moment Ryan came in, clean and freshly shaven, his hair still wet from washing. 'There you are, I was just telling Beth you must show her the chapel later today.'

'Yes, of course. That bacon smells good, Ruth. You're a dab hand with breakfast—we could have done with you at the cottage when we were existing on Greek sausages and fish.'

'Ah, go on! Two's company, three's a crowd. I'll bet you enjoyed yourselves thoroughly.' She winked at Beth. 'Ryan's one of life's organisers—as you may have found out by now. I imagine you were quite comfy.'

'Please, you're making me blush.' He didn't look as if

he'd ever blushed in his life, Beth thought as she watched him sit down and pour himself a cup of tea.

'Oh, we were,' said Beth. 'And yes, he does organise.' She gave him a sweet smile as she said it. The undercurrents were well hidden. He stroked Beth's cheek and smiled back.

'I'd not have managed without your help—darling.' He made the word a subtle caress, and his touch on her face was gentle, yet she felt herself go pink. The irony was there in the inflection in his voice. She wanted to move away, or hit him, she wasn't sure which. Ruth had her back to them, busily engaged in transferring bacon to hot plates under the grill, and Beth fought temptation briefly, and lost. She moved her face slightly and bit his hand. The satisfaction was brief, wiped away at the expression on his face as he took his hand swiftly away. His eyes went as hard as flint, and he looked at her, and the look said it all. Just wait. She closed her eyes.

Then he laughed. 'Ruth, are those old books about Witchwood still in the library? Beth was asking me about them.'

'Why, yes—take her along and show her now, if you like. The breakfast will be another five minutes, I've egg and tomatoes to do yet.'

'Rightoh. Come on, Beth—I know how keen you are.' He stood up and took Beth's arm, very gently, very affectionately, and what did she do now? Scream and run? Numbly, she let him lead her out, along the passage, turn right at the end, and his hand was still on her arm, then he opened a door and pushed her into a large gloomy book-filled room, and closed and locked the door behind him.

'Right, you little bitch,' he said. 'You'll pay for that.' She backed away. He looked capable of anything at that moment. 'What if Ruth comes——' she began, whispering, frightened.

He smiled. It was not a pleasant smile. 'Why, my love, she'll think we've locked *it* because we want to be locked in each other's arms—as every honeymoon couple do—and she'll go away chuckling to herself.' He advanced towards her.

Beth backed behind a table and watched him. 'I won't do it again——' she began.

'Too damned right you won't! Because I'm going to give you the biggest walloping you're ever likely to have—and when you can't sit down they'll think it's for a different reason, and smile at each other knowingly——'

'You can't—you said you wouldn't hit me——'

'Oh, it won't show, I promise you.' He lunged at her and caught her, and carried her, struggling and hitting out, over to the window, sat down on a chair and spanked her with no gentleness at all.

CHAPTER–FIVE

He had a heavy hand, and he used it. Then he stood her up and as she rubbed her tingling backside and the tears of pain and temper pricked her eyes, he said softly : 'And that's only for starters. Any more tricks and I'll do it harder still.' He stood and surveyed her, arms akimbo. 'Nothing to say?'

'I detest you!'

'I'm sure you do. But you really shouldn't go around biting people, you know, it's not civilised.'

'And you are, I suppose?' She wiped a treacherous tear away.

'More than you, apparently. Now we'll go back and eat our breakfast like a happy little pair of honey-mooners, and——'

'Take your hand off me!' She shook it away from her arm. 'I can still *walk*.' She turned and went towards the door and unlocked it, and Ryan followed. He was laughing softly.

Beth made a big effort to appear normal when they reached the kitchen, where Ryan said cheerfully : 'Couldn't find them. Still, we'll look later.'

'Just as well. It's all ready, sit down, my dears.'

Ryan pulled a chair back for Beth. She sat down, hiding a wince in a cough. She *hurt*. The three of them ate, and afterwards Beth did the washing up while Ruth vanished with Adam's breakfast. Ryan said : 'I'm going to read—I'll be in the library if you want me.' He crossed to where Beth stood at the sink. 'In the library—come in if you want me for anything.'

'I won't,' she said, stony-faced, not turning round.

'No? Pity.' He patted her on the behind. 'Oh, sorry—did that hurt?' and began to laugh as he walked away. That did it. Beth was rinsing out a cup with the hot soapy water, and she turned and flung it over him, catching his neck and shoulders with it. The next second he had grabbed and held her, whirled her to face him, pressed her hard against the sink, took hold of her hair in one hand so that she was literally unable to move, and then—the cup dropped on to the floor and shattered, and he kissed her with a savage intensity, his body hurting her with its hardness, because she could scarcely breathe, and her head was being forced back, and she wanted to scream but couldn't, because his mouth covered hers and bruised it with the force of his violence—and she felt her senses reel, and knew she was going to faint, and thought that rape could not be as bad as this—and the room spun round, and as he released her, she fell.

He hauled her up. 'And *that's* just for starters too,' he whispered, his voice even more violent for that. 'I'd hate to tell you what else I can do when I want—but you'll certainly find out if you're not very careful!' And he walked out and left her.

Beth collapsed into a chair and hugged her arms round her body. She knew she couldn't stay like that. She knew she had to be busy when Ruth returned, but for the moment she could do nothing. She was incapable of moving. She was beyond crying, beyond pain. He had hurt her, and she ached with it, but she knew, deep down, that she had got precisely what she had asked for.

Moments passed, she found the power to move, and went over to the sink again. She had finished the washing up when Ruth returned. Ruth took one look at her, and said: 'Oh, you don't look well—what is it?'

Beth managed a weak smile. 'I've a splitting headache,' she admitted, which was true.

'Oh, my dear, you must go and lie down for a while. Go on, there's nothing to do. Where's your husband?'

'In the library.'

'Well, I'll look after him till Adam gets up. Off you go. Here, take a couple of aspirins.' She went to a cupboard and shook two from a bottle. 'There you are. Poor thing!' She patted Beth's shoulder. 'You've been through a lot, getting snowed up and all. I don't think men appreciate these things. A little sleep will do you good. I'll call you before lunch.'

'But I feel awful, letting you do all the work——'

'Nonsense! That's no trouble at all. Off you go now. I insist.'

Beth went. She lay in bed and pulled the covers up, and closed her eyes, trying to shut out the memory of what happened. It was useless. Ryan's face rose to mock her, his expression hard, and his eyes—his eyes dark and cruel, yet laughing at her. She moaned softly. She had thought she was beginning to love him. How wrong she had been, how very wrong! He was worse than all the rest put together, far worse.

She fell into a fitful doze, heard the door opening after what seemed like only a few minutes, and wondered why Ruth should have come up so soon.

But it wasn't Ruth, and it wasn't only a few minutes. It was Ryan to tell her that lunch was ready—sent up by Ruth, who no doubt thought she was doing Beth a favour. He stood at the foot of the bed looking at her. 'Better now?' he said, and there wasn't the slightest trace of sympathy in his voice. 'Lunch is ready—and when we've eaten we're going out to get the car. Remember?'

'I hadn't forgotten.' He clearly thought she had come to bed feeling sorry for herself, seeking attention. Anything she said to try and explain her headache, and Ruth's insistence, would only make it worse, so she didn't even try. She flung back the covers and stood up, smoothing out the creases in her trousers. She slipped her shoes on. 'I'm ready.'

'Want me to carry you?'

She walked past him without a word, opened the door, and went out. On the way down she had time to put a pleasant, happy-after-a-rest and feeling-much-better expression on her face. It wasn't easy, but it worked. Lunch was an enjoyable meal, the food excellent, the conversation flowing freely, and Ryan being utterly charming. He's like Jekyll and Hyde, she thought, as she listened to his amusing account of an incident in a Greek taverna. He can switch effortlessly from one side to the other. He should have been an actor—he'd have been knighted by now. And all the time these thoughts passed through her mind, she kept a carefree, listening expression on her face, nodding and smiling, as the others were doing, at all the right moments in the tale.

But it was a relief when lunch was over, even if it meant she would be alone with him. 'You'll show Beth the chapel now,' said Ruth, as they cleared the plates from the table.

'I will. Come on, Beth, warm coat and boots on. We'll not be long, Adam—will you be having your rest?'

'Very probably. Depends how long you are.' Her grandfather smiled at Beth. 'Don't let him have you driving the tractor now!'

She laughed. 'I won't. See you later.' She felt a warm bond with this man who had so recently entered her life. It was equally clear that he found her company enjoyable. But at times, when she looked at him unobserved, she saw how tired he looked, and her heart ached for all the wasted years when she hadn't known....

They went out the back, and the air outside was warm compared to their own icy aura of frozen politeness. When they were out of sight of the kitchen door, and walking towards the outbuildings across a snow-covered cobbled yard that was treacherous underfoot, Ryan spoke: 'I drive the tractor, you follow,' he said. 'Understand?'

'Yes.' She didn't even look at him. He swung open a large door in a stone building to reveal a small farm tractor. She stood aside and waited. The machine throbbed into life and came slowly out, the huge wheels cutting through the snow leaving deep treads. She followed at her normal walking pace. There was a large metal attachment at the front which effectively shovelled the snow to each side, making it easier to follow. She watched him at the wheel and thought, I'll bet he can fly a plane as well, and drive a bus, and hang-glide, the over-confident swine.

They were half way down the drive when he stopped and switched off the motor. For one absurd moment Beth feared he had read her thoughts and was coming down to give her another good hiding.

'This way,' he said.

'Where? Why——'

'You want to see the chapel? It's this way.' He plunged into the trees where the snow was hardly any depth at all. Only the trees themselves were burdened. She followed reluctantly, not wanting *him* to show her anything, but knowing Ruth or Adam would ask. It was only a short distance from the drive, in a snowy clearing, a simple granite building with yellow stained glass windows. Ryan pushed the door open and went in.

It was cold inside, and only small, with six rows of pews, a simple wooden altar, and a brass crucifix. Beth felt a stirring of some emotion within her, and walked slowly down the short centre aisle while Ryan remained standing by the door. This then was the family chapel, used by generations of Lindens and their servants, and perhaps her own father had worshipped here. She didn't know, but the possibility was there, and it was enough. She wanted to cry, but not in front of him. He would never understand, not in a million years.

Someone had left a hymn book on the front pew seat. She picked it up, and written on the flyleaf, in a rounded childish hand, was 'Adam Linden, 1930.' A lump came into her throat. Her father's book, and it had been here all this time, perhaps waiting for her to find it. She held it to her, and silent sobs wrenched her body, but she didn't turn, she didn't move. She wanted to take the book with her, and perhaps one day she would, but it was not the time now, not yet. She put it down on the seat exactly where she had found it, turned, and walked back towards the waiting man.

'Thank you,' she said, 'for showing this to me. Shall we go now?'

'What was it?' He asked, and he wanted an answer.

'A hymn book that belonged to my father,' she said, and lifted her head proudly. 'It's been here a long time.' She walked past him and went outside. Not even Ryan could take that moment from her. She stood waiting for him, and it seemed to take him an age to follow her and close the door after him, but she hadn't looked back, merely waited, looking towards the drive.

'Let's go,' he said, and she walked on. When they reached the gate where his car stood, he handed her the keys. 'Can you drive my car to the house?' he asked. 'I'll turn this round and you'll follow.'

'Yes.' She unlocked the driver's door and got in, watched him reverse the clumsy vehicle, gave him a good start, and began to drive slowly after him. The job had been done, and with the minimum of fuss, and now they were going back to rejoin her grandfather and Ruth. She wondered when Ralph would arrive. She also wondered how much longer she could go on before she told Ruth the facts. Later that day, she had the answer to both questions.

Her first question was answered that evening. Dinner was over, Ryan and her grandfather were playing chess in the drawing room, Ruth was knitting and watching the two men, and Beth had gone up to her room to wash her lingerie. She had no intention of burdening Ruth with any extra work, and there was an excellent radiator in the bathroom, and she didn't really care if Ryan objected or not.

The task done, she dried her hands and went out of the bedroom and started to walk along the passage. A man stood at the end, and turned at the sound of her footsteps. He was tall, and he was handsome, with a smooth perfection of features, short curly hair, and well chiselled mouth—the kind of face seen on the more successful male model in advertisements. Beth knew who he was—and she also knew, instantly, why Ryan didn't like him. He was also a type she recognised well. She had, after all, fought enough of them off—but it didn't detract from the undoubted charm they possessed. He smiled, and it was a perfect smile, one that had probably been well rehearsed in a mirror to give that exact impression of boyish, modest charm.

'*Hello*!' he said, and the word was a caress, implying delighted surprise.

'Hello. You're Ralph?'

'I am. Forgive me for asking, but are you real or merely a beautiful figment of my feverish imagination?'

She laughed. 'I'm real. I'm staying here. Haven't you spoken to Ruth?'

'My aunt? Not yet. I heard voices from the drawing room and came up to make myself tidy before presenting myself. I've just had an unforgettable journey home.' He didn't need any tidying up. He looked as though he had stepped right out of a catalogue for the more expensive men's clothes. Deep blue velvet jacket, knife-creased grey slacks, a white rollnecked sweater. He looked down apologetically at himself. 'Forgive me for looking such a sight.'

Oh, but you don't, she thought, and you know it. Torn between deflating his ego—which badly needed a dent in it—and flattering him, she chose the latter. Because Ryan didn't like him—and *she* didn't like Ryan—and it could be interesting. 'Heavens, you look perfectly fine to me,' she responded with wide-eyed innocence. 'I'm Beth, by the way. I'm here with Ryan Drago.'

He didn't exactly freeze, but the smile cooled somewhat, and she saw him looking at her left hand, where the ring burned into her finger. 'Ah—yes. You're not——'

'We're married,' she said gently.

'Ah.' He looked at her, and the smile was ever so slightly reproachful, but he was going to be brave about it. 'Then he's to be congratulated.' He looked her lazily up and down, and when his eyes were on her face again Beth allowed a glimmer of coquetry to show in her eyes.

Two could play at this game, and she knew how to flirt, probably better than he, because he was too wrapped up in himself. He caught the glint, and smiled, probably well satisfied. And so am I, she thought, but you don't know why.

'I'm just on my way down,' she said, and managed to convey that it would be nice if she didn't go alone.

'Then I will escort you,' he responded gallantly. 'Can't have you getting lost, can we?'

'You're too kind,' she murmured. 'The house is rather large. I'm only just finding my way about.'

'When did you arrive?'

'Yesterday. We were snowed up for a couple of days in a cottage on the way here.' She wondered fleetingly how he would have coped. She could hardly begin to imagine. As they went down the stairs she stumbled, and he caught her arm.

'Thank you.' She did something that was rather naughty, she knew, but somehow she didn't care. She made her voice rather breathless, as if his touch was disturbing her. 'You see, it was just as well you came down with me.' His touch was anything but disturbing to her. It had the opposite effect, in fact, but Ralph responded by squeezing her arm subtly, the pressure barely noticeable, nothing she could have been offended at, but there all the same. They reached the hall and he walked ahead to open the door for her, his eyes upon her. They were a pale blue in colour. She didn't like pale blue eyes in a man. She acknowledged the gesture with a smiling nod, and went in. Ralph followed her. Ruth turned first, saw him, and jumped up.

'Ralph! When did you arrive?'

He kissed her cheek, 'Hello, darling. Just now. I was sneaking up to my room to freshen up when I met Beth,

so I came down again.' He nodded to the other two
men. 'Hello, Adam, Ryan.'

'Have a good journey?' asked Adam.

'Not too bad. Most of the major roads are clear now.'
He smiled warmly at Ryan and crossed over to him,
hand out. 'Congratulations.'

Ryan stood up, and they shook hands. There was
nothing to give his feelings away. He returned Ralph's
smile. 'Thanks.'

Ruth said: 'They'll be here for the wedding. And
Beth's going to be my matron of honour, isn't that nice?'

'Absolutely marvellous.' Ralph turned the boyish smile
on Beth again.

'You'll want some food,' said Ruth. 'I saved some meat
because I thought you might turn up.' She went towards
the door, and Ralph followed. As they went out, Beth
heard him start to say:

'I would have phoned, but the only telephone box
I tried was out of order——' The voice faded. Beth looked
at Ryan, engrossed in the game again, and went to sit
down. So now she knew Ralph, and she knew exactly
why Ryan had warned her—and why he had said their
'marriage' would protect her. The only thing wrong with
that logic was that Ralph was the kind of man she could
deal with at any time at all—Ryan wasn't. She wondered
what was going on in Ryan's mind, and when he looked
up briefly at her, as Adam pondered a move, she found
out. What she saw in his eyes was well controlled, but
not to be mistaken. It was a deep anger, and she knew it
was directed at her. I don't care, she told herself, and
walked over to sit on the arm of the settee, at the side
of her grandfather.

'May I watch?' she asked.

Adam looked up. 'Of course. Do you play, Beth?'

'Mmm—yes. Not very well.' She smiled warmly at him.

'Then we must have a game after this. I suspect Ryan lets me win sometimes, to humour me.'

'I don't,' denied Ryan. 'You crafty old devil! It takes me all my time to beat you.'

The old man laughed, well pleased, and Beth looked over his head at Ryan, and smiled. It wasn't a warm smile at all. It was a smile to let him know she found his reaction to Ralph's arrival amusing. The drink cabinet was open, and Ryan had a half filled glass at the side of him, and Beth said:

'May I have a drink, please?'

'Of course,' said Adam. 'Ryan?'

'What would you like, Beth?' Ryan stood up and looked at her.

'Oh, gin and tonic, I think—thanks.'

He handed her the filled glass. 'Anything else?' It was said in perfectly courteous tones, but his eyes belied his words.

She sipped. 'That's lovely. Thank you.' He went and sat down again without another word. When Ruth and her nephew returned, Beth was on her second drink, and she had come to a decision. The only person who needed protection from sudden shock was her grandfather, Adam Linden, and it was solely because of this that she had agreed to the bizarre arrangement with Ryan. That, and his idea of protecting her from a wolf. She had met the wolf and she didn't need anyone's protection—certainly not Ryan's. And now, as soon as possible, she was going to tell Ruth the truth. She knew already that she was a kind, gentle soul—she also knew that she could not continue the farce much longer, and especially sharing a bedroom with Ryan. His behaviour

earlier had been unforgivable. The veiled threat after
his second assault still had the power to chill her. His
words: 'I'd hate to tell you what else I can do when I
want—but you'll certainly find out if you're not careful'—left no room for doubt in the imagination. He was
infinitely stronger than she—stronger in fact than most
men, and one wrong word from her could well set off a
violent chain reaction that could end in disaster—for her.
She couldn't live on that kind of tightrope for the rest of
her stay.

The opportunity came later when, at nine-thirty, Ruth
looked at the clock and said: 'I'll go and get a bit of
supper for us all. It's late, Adam.'

'I know,' he waved a hand, engrossed in a game with
Ryan, after two with Beth. 'Don't fuss, I'm enjoying
this. I may beat him.'

Ruth looked at Beth and smiled. 'I'll come and help
you,' Beth said, and followed her out. She waited until
they were in the kitchen, then said:

'Ruth, I've got something to tell you.' Ruth looked
calmly at her and nodded, seeing her white face, the
strain in her eyes.

'I know something's up, love,' she answered. 'But I
don't know what it is. Sit down and I'll make us a
coffee. It won't hurt them to wait for supper a few
minutes.' She put the kettle on and turned to Beth. 'Tell
me.'

So Beth told her everything, right from the beginning,
and the sense of relief as she told it was almost overwhelming. Ruth listened and absorbed, only warm concern showing as the words poured out.

Then the tale was told, and there was silence for a
few moments, then:

'Ah, my dear, I knew, I just *knew* something was

amiss.' She sighed. 'But you feel better now, don't you?'

Beth managed a wan smile. 'Yes. I *had* to tell you, don't you see? It's like a battle all the time—I can't stand it——'

'I know. First things first. Adam mustn't know you're his granddaughter—not yet anyway. Ryan is right in that aspect of it—but I'm glad you are, my dear. When he's stronger he can be told.' She gave a gentle smile. 'And of course we must move you—or him. There's a nice room further along the corridor that he usually has. There's no possibility of Adam finding out, because he sleeps downstairs. We're having one of those chair-lifts fitted soon, but until then he can't go near a staircase.' She sighed. 'I'm quite disappointed in a way. You seemed to go well together when you arrived! But having said that, I've not been unaware of a certain something in the air today. Don't worry, we'll take their supper in, and you and I can go off and sort out your rooms.'

She began to butter bread. Beth heard a slight noise from outside the kitchen, and turned to listen in case someone was coming in, but it wasn't repeated and she forgot about it. She found out much later what had caused it.

They had supper, Adam was taken off to bed by Ryan, and Beth and Ruth stood up. Ralph looked up. 'Leaving me on my own?' he said. 'That's nice!' And he looked at Beth, and he smiled, and she didn't know what she saw in his eyes, but she didn't like it.

'Only for a while,' Ruth answered briskly.

He picked up a magazine. 'I'll have an early night anyway. I'm tired.'

When they were in the bedroom Ruth looked around. 'Well,' she said, 'who's to move—you or him?' She smiled warmly at Beth. 'Of course—most of his things are in that other room anyway. He stays so often he leaves his clothes here. I'll go and put the radiator on in there to warm it up for him.'

'Thanks, Ruth.' Beth went over and hugged her impulsively. 'I'm glad you're going to be my grandmother.'

'So I am!' Ruth looked surprised. 'I hadn't thought of that! Well, well——' She began to laugh. 'It's all happening at once, isn't it?'

'Do you mind if I stay up here?' Beth asked her. 'I know it's early, but I don't feel like facing—him—again tonight.'

She had told Ruth only the barest details of their two fights that day, glossing them over slightly. And about Ryan's warning concerning Ralph she had said absolutely nothing.

'Of course, love. Only one problem—er—how do we break it to him that he's no longer married—and been moved out?'

Beth hadn't thought of that. They looked at each other, dismayed. 'Oh,' said Beth.

'Mmm,' said Ruth. 'Look, I'll go down now, and tell him you'd like a word and you're up here. It's got to be done, and it's better coming from you.'

'I know. I wouldn't expect you to, anyway. It's my problem.'

'Not any more it's not. We're sharing the secret now, remember?'

'Thanks, Ruth.' Tears filled Beth's eyes. 'Oh, don't mind me——' she sniffed. 'It's just—it's nice to feel not alone, if you know what I mean.'

'I know.' Ruth patted her arm. 'Goodnight love, sleep well—and don't worry.' with that, she was gone.

Alone, Beth wandered restlessly over to the window. She wasn't sure of Ryan's reaction. He should be pleased.

The only acting he would now have to do would be in front of Adam. But somehow, although she tried to reassure herself with this thought, it failed to comfort her. She had the feeling he would be angry. And she had seen him angry too often now to be looking forward to it with anything but apprehension.

The minutes passed, and with them her tension grew. Perhaps he wouldn't come up at all. He might just go along to his room—perhaps Ruth had changed her mind and told him—she was as jumpy as a cat on hot bricks. She paced up and down, and time stretched tautly until she could bear it no longer. She went into the bathroom and ran a bath. That would soothe her at least. The previous one had been disturbed by him; she would make sure that this wasn't. She undressed in the bathroom and wrapped a towel round herself, sarong fashion, and went to the bedroom to find her nightie. As she bent over the bed, the door opened and Ryan walked in.

'Oh!' Startled, she grabbed the towel and held it firmly at the top. 'You should have knocked!'

'Why?' He walked across towards her, closing the door before he did so. 'We're married, aren't we? Or are we?' The last three words hung in the air in a dreadful silence. He had caught her off balance by coming in as he had, and she was vulnerable, clad only in a bath towel that, however large and adequate, was hardly the most secure garment.

'Let me get my dressing——' she started to move away.

'No. We'll talk now—like that—as you are.' His eyes touched her with their contempt. 'Perhaps you thought— or hoped—it was Ralph coming in.'

'How dare you! I——'

'I dare. Do you think I didn't see the way you looked at him? My God, if you weren't asking for it——'

Beth couldn't help herself. She couldn't stop herself. She hit him hard, and whirled away to run, to hide, but he caught her, and the towel, already loosened, dropped from her to the carpet.

'Oh, my God!' Gasping, she bent to pick it up, to pull it in front of her, then she realised that he wasn't moving, that he was looking at her, his eyes upon her body—she held it round her, and she was trembling with the fear of what he would do. Because what was in his eyes was unmistakable.

Ryan turned away. 'You'd better get something on.' His voice was very harsh. She fled into the bathroom and put her dressing gown on, belted it firmly and went back into the bedroom. He was still standing there, and he turned slowly, and she knew that the situation was potentially more dangerous than anything that had gone before. He was holding himself in check, but only just. She had seen the naked desire in his eyes, and if he chose to make violent love to her she would be able to do nothing to stop him. She measured the distance to the door.

'I'm not going to rape you.' It was as if he could read her thoughts. 'I came up to find out what it is you have to tell me. I didn't know you'd be prancing around naked or I would have knocked.'

She felt herself flush. 'I've told Ruth the facts about us,' she said, 'and this is no longer your room. Is that clear enough for you? My grandfather and Ralph needn't know, only Ruth—and that should make it easier all round.'

'I see. It certainly makes it easier for Ralph.'

'He doesn't know——'

'Doesn't he?' he cut in. 'He went out at suppertime,

after you and Ruth had gone out. That was when you told her, I gather?' He stared down at her stony faced. 'He said he was going to help. He's never done that before.'

She stared at him blankly. The noise she had heard outside the kitchen—her blood ran cold at the thought of someone silently listening at the door. And Ralph hadn't come in to help. He must have been about to enter when he had heard them talking. She sat down on the bed.

'Nothing to say? You soon will have—to him. I should imagine he doesn't take "no" for an answer—and you must be aware of the way he's been looking at you, even when he thought we were married.'

'He doesn't frighten me,' she shrugged.

'He doesn't intend to. He wants to get you in bed——'

'Get out of here. This is my room now.' She didn't look up at him as she said it, and her voice was expressionless.

'I'll go when I've finished with you.' Ryan pulled her to her feet. 'You thought you weren't safe with me, but you'll wish I was here in the night when you're lying awake waiting for the door to open——'

'No! I'll block the door——'

'What with? A chair? You think that'll put him off?'

'You're exaggerating!' She lifted her chin. 'You're saying it to frighten me just because I don't fancy *you*—don't worry, I saw your face when my towel dropped off—I've seen that look before. I know what *you* want!' She glared at him defiantly. 'You're not as self-controlled as you think—you're just like all the rest!'

'And you'd know about that, wouldn't you? How many men have you had?'

'What do you mean!' she gasped.

'You know damned well what I mean! Don't give me that little-girl innocent look. My God, you had me fooled!'

She pummelled him with her fists, all control gone. 'Stop it! Shut up, you utter beast—you're absolutely——'

'Save it for him,' he grated, and held her so that she couldn't move her arms. 'He won't like his beauty being marred by one of your swift uppercuts—that might make him think twice about——'

'Get out! I can manage *him*!' She glared at him, face pink with exertion.

'Can you? You'll have the chance to find out.' His eyes raked her body, so that she felt naked again. Then he smiled slowly. 'He's welcome. I like my women with a bit of meat on—you're too skinny.' He turned and walked out of the room. He had begun to laugh. Beth flung a slipper at the door. It was the laughter that had finally done it. Right, she thought, I'll show *you*! She wasn't sure yet how she intended to teach him a lesson, but he certainly needed one. She swept into the bathroom, slammed the door and locked it.

CHAPTER SIX

MONDAY morning dawned, and Beth awoke early to realise that she had had a good night's sleep, entirely undisturbed by nocturnal visitors. She had wedged her door with a chair anyway, after Ryan's dire threats. And that had been all they were, she knew now. Just to make her feel uneasy. She got out of bed and went to remove the chair, just in case Ruth turned up for any reason. Another day, and she was going to spend as much time as possible with her grandfather—he had, after all, been the only reason for her visit. She washed and dressed, made up carefully, then inspected herself in the mirror. She had put on a woollen dress in a rust colour. It was belted at the waist, setting off her trim figure to perfection. With it she wore dark tights and high-heeled shoes. The result was eminently satisfactory. She smiled a little smile and turned away, picking up her bag from the chair, then went downstairs.

Ruth was in the kitchen making tea. She looked up. 'My, you look nice today,' she commented. 'Just in time for tea.'

'Thank you,' said Beth. 'I've come to help you get breakfast.'

'No need. There's plenty of time——'

'But I can't let you do all the work,' she protested.

'Listen, love, we usually have a woman from the village to cook and help generally. It's only since we've been snowed up I've been doing it, and I enjoy cooking. So don't try and spoil my fun!'

Beth laughed. 'You've talked me out of it.' She sighed and sat down.

'Oh dear, what was that for? Was Ryan difficult when you told him?'

'Extremely.'

'They all are, at times,' Ruth said wisely. 'I think it's just that they like to think they make all the decisions. Something to do with the male ego.' She sniffed. 'And Ryan is not your ordinary run-of-the-mill man, as you'll have already gathered. But please—don't let anything be amiss when Adam's around, will you?'

'Heavens, no!' exclaimed Beth. 'You've no worries on that score, I promise.'

'Good. That's the important thing.' Ruth looked towards the window. 'Looks like it might clear now in a day or so. Then things can get back to normal, thank goodness. We won't be stuck in the house all the time. You know you're welcome to stay as long as you like, don't you?'

'Thank you,' Beth said quietly.

'You're part of the family—and one day, when it's right, we'll be able to tell Adam. Have you any ties in London? Any family?'

Beth told her the full story, while they drank their tea, and Ruth listened, her eyes gently sympathetic. 'Mmm, I can understand you wanting to come up here as soon as you knew. Your aunt sounds a dragon—oh dear, you've not had a very happy life, have you?'

'It's not been all that bad,' Beth answered quietly. She shrugged. 'But it's nice to know I have a relative of my own. I don't know why my father and uncle left home all those years ago—but having met my grandfather, I can only see a kind and gentle man.'

'He is now. He's mellowed with the years, my dear,

but he used to have a fiery temper, so it's quite possible there were clashes. Who knows? He never talks about his sons, and I don't ask. What's past is past. Now is what matters.' Ruth smiled. 'He's been very ill. It was touch and go at one time, but he pulled round, and now, providing he takes life easy, he has many more years ahead of him. I've known him for twenty years. My late husband and he were good friends. I love him dearly and he's been kindness itself to Ralph and me.'

'Ralph is your nephew, isn't he?'

'Yes. We couldn't have children, and when my sister died shortly after he was born, we adopted him. His father was a regular soldier and couldn't cope with a young child. He married again later and lives in Australia now.'

Beth felt a twinge of sympathy for the other woman. Her life hadn't been a bed of roses either. She began to appreciate even more Ryan's insistence that her grandfather should be unaware of who she was. He clearly had a strong affection for Ruth as well as Adam. 'Ryan is very fond of you, you know,' she told her.

'And I of him.' Ruth laughed. 'He's like another son to me——' she stopped, and Beth saw something that might or might not have been pain in her eyes. Then it was gone. She went on briskly: 'This is in a way his only home since——' she hesitated.

'He was married, wasn't he?'

'Yes. Did he tell you? He never talks about it.'

'No, but I found a photo in his car when I went out for something for him. And you said something about him being married again, just after I'd arrived.'

'He married a Brazilian girl about fourteen years ago. She'd been his assistant on some expedition down the Amazon. They lived there for a while, and had a son——

and both his wife and son were killed in a train crash when they were on their way to meet him in Rio about eight years ago.'

Beth drew in her breath sharply, immeasurably shocked. 'Dear God!' she whispered, closing her eyes.

'He's travelled the world since then, working, working, never stopping. Sometimes when he comes here he sleeps for twenty-four hours. It's as if he's driving himself because there's nothing else to live for.' Ruth looked at Beth with tear-filled eyes. 'So you see that's why I was so delighted when I thought that you and he were——' she stopped, unable to go on, and Beth laid her hand over Ruth's.

'Please don't upset yourself,' she whispered. 'I'm sorry——'

'Tush!' Ruth made an effort to pull herself together. 'It's not *your* fault!' She blew her nose. 'You just looked so ideal together—as if you belonged.'

She was wrong there, terribly wrong, but Beth didn't say so. Something had happened inside her. She no longer wanted to teach him a lesson—that desire had been wiped away in just those few moments of hearing the truth. It explained so much about Ryan, his character, his aggression. Instead, in its place came another sensation, one of warmth. She looked at Ruth.

'Thank you for telling me,' she said. 'I've been—pretty awful to him, I suppose. Now I understand why he's like he is, I'll be different.'

There came footsteps and Ruth made a warning gesture with her finger over her mouth. Beth nodded. Then Ryan walked in. He wore pyjamas and dressing gown, he was unshaven, and he looked as if he hadn't slept. He also looked startled at seeing them.

'Oh. Morning. I came to see—is there any tea?'

'Morning, Ryan. Of course. Sit down.' Ruth went for a beaker, and Ryan sat down at the table. Beth looked at him and her heart ached. He seemed almost ill. Yet what could she say? The gulf between them was too wide ever to breach. She felt the tension in the room, and knew she was part of it. Ruth bustled about, making fresh tea, offering toast, dispelling it as best she could, and Beth thought, we can't go on like this—but we have no choice. It's too late now.

'Thanks, Ruth.' Ruth looked at Beth over his head, and she was puzzled, you could tell.

'Are you all right, Ryan? You look tired.'

'I'll be all right,' he answered shortly. His eyes met Beth's, and they were like stone. He hates me, she thought, and I can't blame him. I thought I hated him too—only I know I don't. She took a deep breath, and he stood up. 'I'll take this upstairs if I may,' he said. He didn't wait for Ruth's reply, but walked out.

She looked at Beth. 'Oh, my God,' she said softly, 'he looks terrible.' She sat down in the chair he had vacated and looked in anguish at Beth.

'It's probably my fault,' responded Beth bitterly. 'We've been battling non-stop ever since we met each other.' She shook her head. 'I'm so mixed up, I can't think straight.'

'Why don't you go and sort it out?' said Ruth.

'How? He detests me—he's as good as said so.' Beth put her head in her hands. 'He'd throw me out of his room——'

'He doesn't look capable of throwing anything.'

'What would I say?' Beth raised her eyes to look at the older woman.

'Go in—tell him—tell him it's senseless to fight, that you want, for your grandfather's sake, to get on well—see what he says. You can but try.'

Beth gave a wry smile. 'If I come bouncing down the stairs with a black eye you'll know it didn't work.'

'But you'll have made the effort, that's what counts.' Ruth patted her shoulder. 'Go on, before you lose your nerve.'

'All right.' Beth went towards the door. 'Cross your fingers.'

'I will. And my toes.'

She ran up to his room and tapped on the door.

'Who is it?'

'It's me—Beth. May I come in?'

'No.'

She waited a moment, then opened the door. It was not an auspicious start to the conversation, but she wasn't going back downstairs to Ruth having admitted defeat. Ryan was sitting on the bed, drinking the tea.

'I said you couldn't come in,' he said flatly.

'I want to talk.' She walked over to his bed.

'I don't. We have nothing to say to each other.'

'Yes, we have.' She sat down facing him on a stool. The curtains were pulled to, and the room was in semi-darkness, which made it easier. His face was darkly attractive, shadowed, and pale. She went on, plunging in before she had time to think too much about it: 'I don't want us to be fighting all the time—can we call a truce?'

He looked up. 'What's the matter? Didn't Ralph rise to the occasion last night?'

She took a deep breath. He was being as deliberately offensive as he could, and her normal reaction would have been swift and angry. But this wasn't a normal occasion. She carried the image of his wife and child too clearly in her mind. 'This has nothing to do with him,' she answered. 'It's only to do with you and me, we're staying here, and we both know that Adam must have no idea we're not married—or who I really am. And wouldn't it be better if we could get on well, not only when we're in his company, but at other times?'

'I don't give a damn either way,' he said. 'He'll never know, I'll make sure of that. He won't see anything amiss.' He looked steadily at her. 'I can put on a good act, just like you can.'

'And Ruth? What about her? She knows what's going on—there's her to consider as well.'

'She can cope.'

Beth took a deep breath. 'Look, I'm trying to apologise,' she said swiftly. 'You're making it damned difficult, though.'

'Is there any reason I should make it easy?' he shot back.

'You could at least listen!'

'I'm listening. I'd just like to know your real reason for this sudden change of heart, that's all. Did she tell you about me—is that it? Did she tell you about my wife and son being killed?' Her face gave her away. He stood up and hauled her roughly to her feet. 'My God!' he said bitterly. 'I don't need your *pity*!'

She stood still. She didn't struggle, she didn't attempt to get away. She looked at him, her eyes wide, her face white with shock. She looked steadily and unflinchingly at him. A kind of inner strength filled her.

'No,' she said softly, 'I don't have pity.'

'Then save your breath,' he said, his voice harsh, 'unless you've come to comfort me in another way——' he ran his hands down her body. She stood perfectly still, and waited. Ryan took his hands away as if they burned.

'Not that either,' she said. 'I told you why I came here.'

'Then go away again.'

'No. I've not finished yet.'

'You just did. Do you want me to throw you out?'

'I'm sure you could, but you won't. I'm not going to fight you back.'

'That would make a change.' He ran his fingers through his hair.

'You're not well,' she said.

'And you feel sorry for me? I'm touched!'

'Why don't you get back into bed?'

'With you?' He laughed. 'Is that an offer?'

'You're being extremely offensive, aren't you?' She smiled as he said it, as though it didn't matter what he said. 'I meant I'd go down and make you some breakfast and bring it up.'

'Your concern is deeply moving.'

'At least it's genuine,' she retorted. 'Which is more than I can say of your so-called witty replies.'

'That's better. You're being almost human now. The ice maiden bit didn't last long, did it?'

'You're impossible!' she snapped.

'You've called me worse than that.'

'I'm trying to keep my temper, but you're making it difficult.'

'I hoped I was making it impossible,' he answered swiftly. 'What else do I have to do?'

'I'm going,' she said, and walked away from him. 'I'm sorry I came——'

'Don't go.' He caught her arm. 'We're just warming up. Don't leave now.'

'Don't push your luck,' she retorted crisply. 'I felt

sorry for you because you didn't look well. There's no-thing wrong with your tongue, though. That's as sharp as ever—perhaps there's nothing wrong with you at all. Did you sleep badly?'

'How did you guess?'

'Well, it could hardly have been with thinking about me,' she answered. 'I'm too skinny, remember?' She laughed. '*Others* don't think so.' Then she put a gentle hand on his and loosened his grip from her arm. She looked into his eyes, saw them narrow, knew she had touched him on the raw. Yet she didn't know why. 'I'm going right now. Just remember, I'll be as pleasant to you as possible. What *you* do is up to you.'

She reached the door, and was opening it when his arm reached out and slammed it shut. He was right behind her, he then twisted her round to face him, pressing her hard against the door, and putting his mouth down on hers in a savage kiss that went on and on. . . .

Beth didn't try to struggle free, because she sensed it would only arouse him further. And in any case, she now knew it was what she had been waiting for all along. . . .

She responded, gently at first, then more fiercely as his own savage passion grew more intense. Locked in his arms, she helpless, knowing she was helpless, and revelling in it, he like a man possessed.

'Oh, God,' she heard his broken murmur, and some small part of her stood aside, coolly watching, knowing that nothing like this had ever happened before, no man had ever wanted her so badly before—and there came a sharp rapping at the door, and Ralph's voice:

'Ryan? Everything all right?'

There was an instant's electric silence, then: 'Yes—fine,' Ryan answered thickly. And in that instant of time Beth came to her senses with the sensation of having icy

water thrown over her. She struggled for balance, heard
Ralph's steps going down the corridor, stared at Ryan,
put her hand to her mouth, aghast at what she was doing
and said :

'Oh God, I must go!'

She turned to the door to escape. Ryan remained
standing where he was as if powerless to move. Then she
opened the door, and fled. She ran into her own room
and stood panting, leaning against the door. She didn't
want to bump into Ralph. She didn't want to see anybody—not for a while, until she had recovered.

She went over to the dressing table and brushed her
hair, staring at her white face in the mirror. She should
never have listened to Ruth. It had been a mistake to
go to Ryan's room, one she would have regretted for
a long time. Because she knew now, at last, who was the
one who lacked control. She had no lipstick on, not
surprisingly. With a shaking hand she applied a fresh
coat, then turned away from the mirror and went to sit
on her bed.

She must never be alone with him again, that much
was certain. And what would he think of her now? His
opinion had been low, to say the least, before. She
shuddered to even think how he must regard her now.
There was only one thing to do, for the sake of her own
self-respect. Put the incident entirely out of her mind.

But that was more difficult than she could ever have
imagined it would be. Ryan didn't come down to breakfast, and she had no opportunity to say anything to Ruth,
because Ralph was in the kitchen when she went down.
He looked at her in a certain way, and she knew at that
moment that he had known she was in Ryan's room.
His manner was perfectly affable, however, as he asked
her how she had slept, and told her he was going into the

village for food, did she want anything fetching back. She assured him she didn't, and they ate breakfast with Ruth in amiable harmony. But once, when she looked at him, and before he was aware of her glance, she seemed to see a satisfied expression in his eyes.

Then he went out. Ruth looked at Beth. 'Well?' she said. 'How did it go?'

And how could I begin to tell her? thought Beth. 'Not too well,' she said, in the understatement of the year. 'But at least I put my point across, that I intended to be very nice—whether he listened or not, I don't know——' and she burst into shaming tears.

'There now, love—oh dear me, they're not worth crying over, you know.' Ruth soothed her in motherly fashion, and Beth sobbed: 'But he—he kissed me—and —and——'

'Ssh, don't tell me anything you'll regret. I'd rather not know.'

'I'm sorry,' Beth sniffed. 'I don't know what's the matter with me.'

Ruth looked at her very sagely, and gave a little smile. 'You wouldn't have fallen for him, by any chance?' she suggested.

Was it so obvious? Beth looked at her in alarm, and Ruth shook her head. 'It's all right, love, it happens. He's a very attractive man. But don't break your heart over him. He'll always be a wanderer, you know. You'll meet someone your own age and settle down, you'll see. I'll bet you have your pick now, don't you?'

Beth pulled a little face. 'But I've never met anyone like him before——'

'That's the trouble. There aren't many like him, and whether that's a good or bad thing, I'm not sure. I was surprised when he married, I must admit, but he did, and he was very happy—until——'. she stopped.

'Did you meet her?'

'Yes. He brought her here, before they'd had their son, it would be. She was a pretty little thing, Eva was her name, and she obviously adored him.' She smiled sadly. 'But it's all in the past now. I saw the change in him afterwards. He became harder—well, you know what he's like. He's a lonely man I suppose, but he never seeks sympathy.'

He had said that to Beth, in the bedroom. Had said fiercely: 'I don't need your *pity*——' before he had so nearly made love to her. And perhaps that was all it had been, an urgent need to be satisfied, to make her forget any thoughts she might have about him. It had nearly worked too. If Ralph hadn't knocked at the door—she shivered. She had mistaken lust for love. She wouldn't make that mistake again. Not with him. Not ever.

She took a deep breath, then smiled. 'Well,' she said, 'he'll be down soon, I dare say. You'll see a change in me as well.'

'I will?' Ruth looked surprised. 'Oh! In what way?'

'You'll see.' Beth gave a mysterious smile. 'All will be pleasant and charming.' she nodded briskly, perhaps to convince herself as well as Ruth, who laughed.

'I'm sure you're never anything else, love.'

Beth didn't even understand herself what had come over her. A combination of various factors, and upper-most pride. She was going to stop reacting to Ryan—she was going to treat him as just another person in the house. In front of Adam obviously in a slightly different, warmer way, but always with her self-possession intact. It was the best way—it was the only way.

She had her chance to put it to the test when Ryan appeared shortly afterwards. She and Ruth were in the drawing room with Adam when the door opened and he walked in. She looked up and gave him a pleasant smile. 'You look better. Shall I get you some breakfast?'

He looked at his watch. 'Well, it's nearly lunchtime. A piece of toast wouldn't come amiss, though.'

'I'll get it,' said Beth, as Ruth started to rise, and she went out. She put a slice of bread in the toaster, found the butter, and waited for the toast to pop up. Ryan walked in and closed the door.

'It's all right, I'll bring it in,' she said pleasantly.

He looked at her. 'I'll have it out here.'

'Right.' She popped the hot toast on to a plate and buttered it. 'Marmalade?'

'No, that'll do.' She handed it to him, then put on the kettle. She was managing to ignore the smothering atmosphere of his mood. 'I'll make you a drink as well,' she said. 'Tea or coffee?'

'Coffee, please.'

'Right.'

'Stop saying "right" in that infuriating manner,' he commented. 'You sound like a schoolteacher.'

She suppressed a beautiful retort. 'I'm sorry, I'll remember not to. Black or white coffee?'

'White.' She made it, handed it to him, then stood back.

'Anything else before I go?' It was getting extremely difficult to keep calm in the overwhelmingly stifling atmosphere, but she was determined to remain so.

'You have nothing else I want.'

'I know,' she answered softly, and went out. When he came into the drawing room a few minutes later she was talking to Adam about various jobs she had had, and it wasn't necessary to speak to or even look at him, but Beth made the effort, including him in the conversation, and he joined in amiably. He was a different man from the one a few hours previously.

It seemed that Ralph was like an interested onlooker—slightly amused, perfectly courteous, yet with an extra quality in his manner that Beth found difficult to analyse. But later she found out what it was.

She had gone into the library after dinner to find a book for her grandfather, and was searching along a shelf when he came in quietly, closing the door behind him. She turned round to see who it was. 'Oh, hello,' she said.

He walked over to her before replying. 'Beth?' he said softly. 'I've been trying all day to talk to you.'

'Have you? I didn't notice.' She smiled gently at him. 'You don't look shy to me.'

'I'm not, usually, but I've never met anyone like you before.' She had heard that many times. He'd have to do better than that. She told him so.

'No, I mean it.' His face was quite serious.

'Mmm. Perhaps it was because you thought I was married, and now you've found I'm not.' She smiled sweetly at him. 'You were listening at the door last night, weren't you? Didn't you know it's a nasty habit?'

'I didn't intend to—honest, cross my heart—but I reached the door just as something quite riveting was said, and yes, I confess it, I stayed to listen.' He hung his head as if ashamed. It was so outrageous it made Beth laugh.

'And you were naturally intrigued?'

'Naturally. It isn't often you get a beautiful bride who turns out to be—not a bride after all.'

'How true!' she sighed. 'I don't make a habit of it, I promise you. There was a good reason.'

'Yes, I know.' His voice was dry. 'Thought out by our *dear* Ryan, no doubt?'

She gave him a very level look. 'He doesn't particularly like you, either,' she said. 'And I'd watch it if I were you. That's a friendly warning. I would think he has quite a temper on him.'

'Oh, you don't need to tell me. Anyway,' he went on, 'I didn't come here to talk about him.'

'What did you come for?'

'Can't you guess?'

'I could make a few, actually.' Beth gave him a pleasant smile and moved away along the shelf. Ralph followed her.

'You intrigue me,' his voice was pitched low. 'You appear not to like him, and yet——' a delicate pause, 'you were in his room this morning.'

'Oh, so you noticed? Yes, I was. I'd gone to see if he was ill, actually. Don't tell me you were listening at that door as well?' She began to laugh. 'You'll get flat ears if you——'

'You didn't seem to be fighting then.'

'No, we weren't. He was kissing me—as if you hadn't guessed. But it's none of your business anyway. I'm over eighteen, and ladies have got the vote now, you know.'

'Damn it!' he exclaimed. 'You're the most maddening woman——'

'There's no need to start insulting me, just because I don't fancy you.' She stared at him. 'Do you expect everyone to fall over themselves whenever they see you? Well, I don't. If you must know I think you're a conceited devil.'

'You fancy him, though? Is it his money that gets you? Is that it?' He was icily furious now, and she would have been amused if she hadn't been so utterly fed up with men in general, and one man in particular.

She glared angrily at him. 'Don't be stupid! I don't fancy anyone, if you must know. You're all the same——'

'I'm not. I'm not like him for a start.'

'Well, bully for you!' She turned away and began to look with intense concentration at a row of books. Ralph whirled her round and caught tight hold of her arms.

'You don't turn your back on *him*, you——'

'Let me go!' She had had quite enough. She elbowed herself free and faced him. 'Buzz off, junior——' She got no further. He caught and kissed her. Furious, she struggled free and slapped him hard.

White-faced, he stared at her. 'You little *tramp*!' he spat out. 'You're just a——'

She hit him again, and he hit her back—and she fell backwards against the shelves. Then Ryan's voice came from the door: 'Touch her again and I'll kill you.'

They had neither of them heard him come in. Beth gasped as Ralph whirled round. Ryan came in, slammed the door shut, and advanced on the white-faced man. 'I mean it,' he said. 'Get out of here now.'

'You can't tell *me* what to do——' began Ralph.

'I just did.' Ryan looked big and dangerous—and quite capable of carrying out his threat. 'If you want to hit anybody, try someone your own size, not a woman. Try *me*,' he added softly.

Ralph's lip curled. 'Big talk,' he sneered. 'And all bluff. You wouldn't chance scaring old Adam.'

'I'd hit you so's it wouldn't show. I wouldn't mark your pretty face, never fear, but by God, you'd hurt for a few days.' And he meant it—and Ralph, now, knew that he meant it. There was a painful silence. Then:

'I'm going. It's hardly worth staying here anyway. You deserve each other.' Ralph walked towards the door. 'I mean—you *really deserve* each other.' Then he had gone.

Beth rubbed her aching jaw where Ralph's hand had landed quite heavily. She looked up at the angry man before her. 'Thanks,' she said.

Ryan gazed at her, eyes colder than she had ever seen. 'I'm damned sure you asked for all you got,' he said, 'and I hope it hurts. I can almost sympathise with him.' He looked at the closed door, then back to Beth. 'I was sent in to see if you needed help with the books, but you were obviously too busy to look.' He smiled thinly. 'You sure do get around, don't you? It's a pity there are no more young male relatives for you to have your little scenes with. It would stop life from getting dull.' He looked her up and down. 'You're quite a girl.'

She turned her back on him and stared at the books in front of her, seeing nothing, only a brown blur. She was not going to answer or retaliate in any way whatsoever. She hated Ralph and she hated Ryan. She waited for him to go, and pretended a great interest in the old volumes. Her jaw ached, but she wouldn't rub it. She saw—by a miracle—the book she was seeking, and lifted it out.

'I'm going back to my grandfather,' she said. 'Are you coming or not?'

He didn't answer, merely walked past her to the door and went out. After a moment's hesitation, Beth followed. Ryan was already half way across the hall when she reached the door. She looked at his retreating back. I wonder why he bothered to rescue me, she thought.

CHAPTER SEVEN

BETH answered the telephone in the hall the following morning, because she was passing it when it rang. A man's voice asked for Mr Lowson and for a moment Beth didn't realise who he meant. Ryan was coming in from the front garden at that moment.

'It's someone for Mr Lowson,' she said.

'That's Ralph. He's upstairs.' Ryan then walked past without another word. She put her tongue out at him.

'Just hold on a moment, will you, please? I'll fetch him.' She ran to the foot of the stairs and shouted Ralph's name, heard his answering yes, and called:

'Telephone!'

'Right.' She walked out into the kitchen. She didn't really care if he came down or not. She hadn't spoken to him since the previous night's appalling scene in the library, and she hadn't intended to speak again. Her chin hurt, and a bruise which she had managed to conceal with make-up made eating a delicate business. She wished now that Ryan had hit him. She had avoided Ryan as much as possible except for that unavoidable hour in the drawing room before Adam had gone to bed. And it had been as though nothing had been wrong.

Ruth was in the kitchen preparing lunch. Beth laughed. 'No one ever told me your surname,' she said. 'A call just came for Mr Lowson and I hadn't a clue who they meant.'

'A call for Ralph? Fancy that.' Ruth smiled at her. 'You can help if you like.'

'Of course—I've told you.'

'Peel some potatoes, love. Then I can get on with this pudding.'

'Will do.' Beth seated herself at the table and began happily peeling. It was nice to feel useful. It was also nice to be in a room where there was no friction. Her only regret was that Ruth, who was so wonderful, should have an adopted son like Ralph. That's life, she thought. She only hoped Ralph would never hurt her. He treated her with a casual courtesy, but that might be for the benefit of visitors. And it was clear that Ruth was very fond of him.

The subject of her thoughts came in at that moment, and Beth looked down at her potatoes and began concentrating on what she was doing.

'Hello, love, was it anyone interesting?' asked Ruth, looking up from her mixing bowl. There was a smudge of flour on her cheek, and she looked very young.

'It was, as a matter of fact.' He paused, presumably to give full dramatic effect to what he was about to say. 'I've just been offered a job in London.'

Even Beth had to look up at that, astonishment mingling with relief—and surprise. It was as if her unspoken wish had had a speedy answer. He stood there smiling —no, it was more a smirk than a smile, but Beth didn't mind that.

'How lovely,' said Ruth, and wiped her floury hands on a cloth. 'Do you have to go for an interview or anything?'

'No. They want me down there in two days. I'd better go and make a couple of calls.' And he nodded almost pleasantly at Beth and made his exit.

Beth didn't really care what the job was—bus driver, frozen food packer—just as long as he wasn't *there*, but manners demanded that she show polite interest. 'You look delighted,' she told Ruth. 'What sort of work does Ralph do?'

'He's done modelling in adverts—you know, man in background for tonic water where he was one of three men at a bar——' No wonder there had been something vaguely familiar about those well sculpted features, thought Beth wryly. And he had looked the masculine model type too. Ryan had never mentioned his job, though. She nodded enthusiastically.

'Perhaps this is a follow-on. Will you miss him?' It almost hurt to say it. She couldn't visualise anyone missing *him*—or Ryan for that matter, but it was only polite.

'Well—normally, yes, of course, but I have Adam now, and children must grow up and move away, mustn't they?'

Indeed yes, thought Beth. Especially children like him. And the further the better. 'London's not far,' she answered brightly, resisting the temptation to do a little dance in celebration.

'True. Well, well, we must find out all about it over lunch.'

Beth finished the potatoes and gathered up the peelings in newspaper. What a coincidence, she thought. What a coincidence that he should be leaving so soon after that near-fight with Ryan—she paused, remembering something.

Ryan had used the telephone extension in the library much later the previous evening. She had been about to go in to return the book, and had heard his voice coming faintly from the room. So she had left it, and returned the book later. He had been laughing, and then he had been speaking very quietly—as if he didn't want to be overheard. It seemed rather odd, because he hadn't mentioned telephoning anyone to Adam or Ruth, which would have been the normal thing to do.

Strange, she thought, and put the idea from her mind as Ruth asked her a question about lunch. But it returned much later.

It was after dinner that evening. They had heard all the details of this marvellous new job which involved a contract with a well known mail order firm to work exclusively for them for a year, and to travel abroad for certain other photographs. And Ruth, sitting knitting next to Adam, asked Ryan: 'Don't you have friends in London connected with that same firm, Ryan?'

He looked up from the magazine he was reading. 'Sorry?'

'I said—don't you have friends connected with this firm Ralph is going to work for?'

'Ah. I do know one of the directors, vaguely,' he replied. 'Used to be at school with him.' He frowned across at Ralph. 'It would be your agent who contacted you, wouldn't it?'

The two men were perfectly civil to one another when either Adam or Ruth were present. And as Beth carefully avoided both at other times she didn't really know—or care—whether they spoke or not.

'Yes,' Ralph nodded. 'Apparently someone in their advertising department had seen my telly commercial and thought I'd be ideal, and had got in touch with Rosen, my agent.' He smiled at his aunt.

Beth's very faint suspicion about Ryan's secret telephone call became slightly more solid. But she said nothing, because there was nothing to say.

Shortly afterwards Adam went to bed, helped out of the room by Ruth. Beth immediately stood up. She wasn't going to stay in there with them. She went out to the kitchen to make coffee, and was filling the kettle when Ryan walked in. She didn't look round, or speak, she began to search for cups and saucers.

'I'm making coffee for everyone,' she said. 'And I can manage on my own.'

'I'm quite sure you can manage lots of things on your own,' he retorted smoothly. 'But I didn't come out to see you, I came out to look at the fridge. Ruth asked me to fix the hinge on the ice drawer.' And he went over to it.

'Do you have to do it now?' she responded.

'Now is as good a time as any.' He looked at her, and his face was hard.

She moved away from the refrigerator after taking out the milk, and went over to the sink. Ryan began to whistle softly, as he crouched in front of the open refrigerator door. She waited impatiently for the water to boil, sensing the inevitable tension building up in the room. And who was worse to be alone with? Him or Ralph? There was hardly anything to choose between them. At least, with Ralph gone, things would be a little easier—she hoped.

He reached over for a screwdriver from the dresser shelf and it fell to the floor with a clatter. He swore softly, and Beth laughed—more as a release from tension than anything else.

'It doesn't take much to amuse you, does it?' he remarked, as he picked it up.

'Nor you——' she retorted, 'the way you were laughing on the phone, last night. It would be a funny coincidence if it was your director friend you'd rung, wouldn't it?'

There was a few seconds' silence, then he stood up slowly and turned to face her. 'What *do* you mean?' he asked softly. And Beth knew at that moment. She knew the truth. But she still wasn't sure why. She shrugged.

'I don't think you need me to spell it out,' she answered, and turned away to attend to the boiling kettle.

'Try anyway—unless, of course, you can't spell.'

'All right.' She was stung by his tone. 'I think you rang someone and fixed it for them to offer Ralph this job. People normally only do things like that if they're very fond of someone—and I don't think you are, really—or to get rid of them.'

He began to laugh. She glared at him. 'Now why would I want to get rid of him?'

'I can think of several reasons. You must have a lot of pull with your director friend.'

'He owes me a favour. Any more questions?'

'No.' She made the coffee. 'But you've answered *my* question.'

'I haven't. All this is supposition on your part.'

'Yes.' Then she smiled very slowly at him, and saw his eyes narrow. 'It's all right,' she said, ever so sweetly, '*I* won't say anything.'

'Do you think I'd care if you did?'

'Knowing you—possibly not. You don't really give a damn about anything or anybody, do you?'

'You wouldn't know. You don't know me.'

'I don't particularly want to. I've seen you in action——'

'Hardly.' It was said in very dry tones, and in a certain way. Beth had not imagined there could be such a wealth of meaning in one word—and found herself going pink. She turned away so that he wouldn't see, and set out the cups with great precision. Damn, damn, *damn*, she thought. He was impossible!

He too turned back to his task, and she poured out the coffee. 'Shall I leave yours here?' she said sharply.

'No. I'll be in in a minute—unless, of course, you want to speak to Ralph in private?'

She didn't bother to answer that. She picked up the loaded tray and went towards the door. 'Need any help?' he enquired, as she struggled to open the door.

She gritted her teeth. 'I can manage——' only she couldn't. The door came open too quickly, caught the tray—and everything crashed, with a resounding shattering clatter, to the floor. She tried vainly to grab, to rescue, stooping—and cut her hand on a shard of a cup. Ryan turned, saw what was happening, came over to where she stood holding her bleeding hand, and gave an exasperating sigh.

'You're a stubborn little creature!'

'Leave me alone! *Ouch*!' This as he took her hand and lifted it to inspect the damage.

'You fool,' he grated. 'Go over to the sink. I'll get the first aid box.'

'I can manage, thank——' she began.

'Shut up. Do as you're told, before you bleed all over the floor,' and he pushed her, not ungently, towards the sink. She went; she had no choice. Her hand bled profusely and to her horror she found herself going faint. He took one look at her ashen face and pulled up a chair to the sink.

'Sit,' he said. She sat.

Ryan opened the tin he had brought from a cupboard, rinsed her hand under the cold tap, then pressed the slit firmly together and applied a wad of medicated gauze. 'Hold that while I open a bandage,' he said.

A minute later she had a very efficiently strapped up hand, and he was washing his. 'Stay where you are,' he said. 'I'm going to clear up the mess before anyone comes in.' This he proceeded to do, putting the broken crockery in a kitchen bin, then mopping the floor, and finally putting down a sheet of newspaper to cover the damp stone. 'And now I'll make more coffee,' he said.

'Thank you for your help,' Beth had no choice. The whole operation had barely taken five minutes, from her disastrous attempt to open the door, to everything being as normal.

'How's your hand?' he asked.

'Throbbing a bit.'

'It would,' he answered, with no sympathy she could detect. Not that she expected any from him. 'But you'll live.'

Ruth came in at that moment, took a look at Beth's white face and even whiter hand, and her eyes widened. 'Oh, Ruth, I'm so sorry,' Beth apologised. 'I had an accident—I'm afraid I've broken some cups and saucers——'

'Never mind *that*. We've loads. What did you do to your hand?'

'Cut it when I tried to rescue the tray I'd knocked flying.'

'You poor thing!' She clicked her teeth, saw Ryan filling the kettle and nodded. 'Making more, Ryan? That's it. Need any help?'

'No, thanks. Go and join Ralph. We'll be in in a minute.'

'Well, if you're sure. We're just deciding what he'll need to take. It's all so sudden, isn't it?' Ruth put her hand to her cheek. 'I'm quite dizzy with it all.' But she looked pleased, all the same, and Beth wondered, fleetingly, if she was in fact relieved at Ralph's imminent departure. She could hardly ask. She began to see that there might be in fact more than one reason for Ryan's move. He loved Adam like a son would—he would want his happiness above everything, and although on the surface her grandfather and Ralph seemed to get on well, she now wondered. Ruth, after a few more words with Ryan on where further crockery was to be found, went out.

'You can open the door for me,' he told Beth as he poured out the four coffees.

'Yes. Don't they get on?'

'Who?' But he knew.

'Ralph and—my grandfather.'

'Well enough.'

'That means nothing.'

'It's not meant to. Are you ready?'

'Yes.' She stood up, went over to the door, and opened it. She had her answer.

As she lay in bed later, she thought over events since she had set out for Witchwood from London. A lot of things had happened. She was now, although still unofficially, part of the family. And what a family! Ryan was not a blood relative yet he seemed the most powerful influence at work. Things happened when he was around. She imagined they always had. And in a strange way, she could not visualise life without him. On that rather odd thought, she fell asleep.

The snow had nearly cleared by the following day, assisted by a strong sun, and a wind that had sprung up overnight and woken Beth with its eerie howling through the trees. She remembered in the morning how she had woken up in the night and gone to the window to hear the wind, to see the darkened trees bending in it. The atmosphere had been eerie and she wondered briefly if there was any legend about the woods which might have led to the house being called Witchwood. By morning she had forgotten it. But the memory returned during the morning when she went out for a walk in the gardens. Clad in warm coat and trousers and boots, she tramped through the densely packed trees and an echo of the night came back to her, and for a moment she shivered as she remembered.

Her imagination was vivid. She could well believe there might have been witches at one time, perhaps long before the house was built. She could almost see them. . . . She began to walk more quickly, dismissing the fancy. But the trees were tall and silent, effectively cutting off the light, and she didn't realise how extensive the grounds were until she found she was totally lost. She was surrounded by trees, trees, and more trees. And the world was now a silent one. She mentally shook herself, chiding herself for the foolish fancies which had gripped her. She only had to walk on until she cleared the wood. That was all. . . . Then she saw a familiar building, and began to laugh, and walk more quickly towards it. The chapel. How *absurd* to have been scared! It was near the drive, but before she went back to the house she would step inside for a few moments, and look around in peace, without *him* watching her from the door.

She pushed open the old wooden door, which creaked alarmingly, and went inside. The sun slanted in through the side windows and the dust eddied and swirled as she disturbed it. The wedding would be here soon, and Beth knew a kind of satisfaction at the idea which occurred to her then. She would come down, armed with buckets and cloths, and give the chapel a much needed cleaning. She ran her fingers along the back of a pew and grimaced at the powdery dust sticking to them. Polish and dusters too; the idea appealed. She sat down at

the front and looked around her slowly drinking it all in.
The book with her father's name in it was beside her. A
scrap of his childhood, left here for her to find after so
many years. Tears filled her eyes, and she blinked them
determinedly away. The past had gone for ever. The
present and the future were what mattered now. And
in a strange way, as she sat there, feeling the peace and
quiet wash over her, she knew she had been meant to
find her grandfather, to come here to Witchwood....
Perhaps even to come and sit in the chapel alone to
realise all those things.

It was time to go. Ruth would be wondering where
she had got to, for an hour had passed, and Beth had not
said how long she would be, but had intended only a
brief search around the gardens. She stood and stretched,
took a last look around, seeing in her mind's eye how
much more beautiful the chapel would be for a loving
polish.

The door opened slowly, she jerked her head round,
then froze. She didn't know who she had expected to
see. Ruth—Ryan perhaps. But not Ralph. He closed the
door behind him and stood there. He wasn't smiling. She
marvelled that she had ever considered him handsome.
His features were petulant, like a spoiled child who has
just been robbed of a favourite toy, and is working up
into a fine temper.

'Well, well,' he said softly. 'Here you are.' Then he
smiled. It would have been better if he hadn't. She much
preferred the petulant expression. 'Just going over things
in your mind?'

'Well, I wasn't thinking about *you*,' she retorted.
'That's for sure.'

'I didn't imagine you were. It would be more—money
matters, wouldn't it?'

Beth didn't know what he meant. She stared blankly at him. 'Oh, very good,' he mocked. 'The wide-eyed innocence is almost convincing—you'll be telling me next you don't know your granddaddy is a very rich old man.'

Then light dawned. In a few brief moments of realisation, she knew exactly what was going on in his mind, and she felt sick. She felt breathless too. She walked towards him. 'Let me pass,' she said, her voice husky with anger. Nothing she said would convince him she cared nothing for her grandfather's money, and she wasn't going to try. He stood leaning against the door and laughed.

'Try and move me,' he suggested.

'Don't be stupid,' she snapped. 'I've already had one encounter with you, and that was enough to last me a lifetime.' She touched her bruised jaw. 'The make-up covers where you hit me. Otherwise Ruth might have wondered——'

'I don't make a habit of hitting women. You asked for it!'

'Of *course* I did!' She blinked as if in surprise. 'Heavens, I'm sure *you're* not responsible for your actions. Thank heavens you're leaving soon, that's all I can say. I hope you get all you deserve!'

'He's done a good job of brainwashing you.' She didn't need to ask who 'he' was—she knew. She laughed.

'I've got better things to do than listen to anyone talking about you. You're a nothing in my book. Are you going to let me pass?'

'Not yet. I've not finished——'

'Well, I have. Why don't you go and finish your packing like a good little boy?' She knew she was on dangerous ground. They were completely alone, well away from the house and any chance of being overheard, but his sickening innuendo about money had stripped her of caution. Ralph's inflated ego was an affront to anyone; he must go through life, she thought, cushioned by his own conceit. Ryan couldn't realise it—or perhaps he could—but his phone call was the best thing he could have made. She only felt sorry for the people Ralph would be working with. But that wasn't her problem.

'They'll be waiting for you in London,' she added, caution returning. 'So why don't you get some practice in—at being pleasant, I mean.'

'I can be so charming, never fear.'

'Oh, I don't fear. I'm sure you can turn it on when necessary—when you want to impress anyone. I'll bet they'll find you a real smoothie.'

'But you don't, of course.'

'How *did* you guess?' Her voice dripped sarcasm.

'I'll give you something to remember me by——' and he suddenly lunged forward and grabbed tight hold of her. Beth had had more than enough, and this time, sub-consciously, she had been ready for him, every nerve in her body a-tingle with anticipation of attack. Her anger gave her an added power too, and with a strength that surprised her, she freed her hands and boxed his ears soundly, hearing his yell of pain as he was momentarily deafened—then she kicked him on the shin, and in the instant that he doubled up she whipped past him, flung the door open, and ran out.

Then she made her mistake. She ran the wrong way. In her confusion she missed the track to the drive, turned to try and correct the mistake, but too late. He was after her, temper up, and she could only run on in the direction she had started, deeper into the trees, twigs catching her clothes as she ran, fear lending speed to her legs. She was lost again, but he was close behind, swearing and cursing, and she knew terror. For if he caught her. . . .

Dear God, she prayed, stumbling, her hand hurting as a branch caught it, making it throb anew, don't let him catch me—there was a clearing ahead, and she remembered it from before, and a branch lying on the ground. She bent and grabbed it, heard his voice, triumphant, from nearby—too near—'You bitch—wait till——' She straightened up, swung round, and he reached her. She landed out with the branch, missed, and he caught it and flung it away. She had a second's respite as he did so and she turned, running—and cannoned into Ryan.

'Ah!' The impact took her breath away. Then Ryan pushed her to one side.

'Get out of the way,' he said. She had never heard him speak like that before. Stumbling, she leaned against a tree, legs weak with shock, and saw Ryan move forward, saw, as if in a kind of daze, that Ralph had half turned as if to escape, as if he realised now. . . . But it was too late. Ryan moved as swiftly as a pouncing tiger, caught Ralph, pulled him round. Then she saw Ralph going down. It was as if it was all happening in slow motion. His legs crumpled like a doll's, then his body went back, his arms flailing limply, then he hit the ground and lay there. Ryan pulled him to his feet. Beth saw the whiteness of Ryan's face, his blazing eyes as he held Ralph upright.

'No!' she shouted, and began to run forward. 'Don't——'

'Don't what? Hit him again?' Ryan mocked, turning his gaze on her. 'I'm going to paste him to the——'

'You'll kill him——' she was sobbing now, and caught Ryan's arm. 'Please!'

Ralph was groggy, but conscious. His face bore no mark, but was ashen. He swayed on his feet, tried to aim a punch in Ryan's direction, but nearly fell. Ryan caught him and swung him round and slapped him hard across his face. Then, holding him by the lapels of his jacket, he snarled: 'I told you what I'd do if you touched her again. It would be like beating a child—I've no taste for that. But I'm telling you now. Keep well away from Beth now and until you leave this house. And say you're sorry to her for whatever you've done.'

Ralph looked at him, his eyes fearful yet defiant. 'Go to hell,' he whispered brokenly. His head jerked back as Ryan hit him again, then Ryan turned to Beth.

'What did he do?' he said. It was a question that demanded an answer.

'He came into the chapel when I was sitting there—we had an—an argument——' she faltered.

'And?'

'He caught hold of me, so I hit him and ran out.'

Ryan pushed the shaking man away from him and turned his back on him. 'Get back to the house,' he said to Beth.

'I don't know where it is. I got lost——'

'You would,' he began, and Beth saw Ralph's upraised arm, saw the branch he held, and yelled out a warning —the branch crashed harmlessly down on to Ryan's shoulder as he moved in the split second of time, then Ryan turned, caught the branch, wrenched it out of Ralph's hands and punched him hard on the jaw. Ralph went down as if poleaxed, and lay still. Ryan rubbed his shoulder and looked down dispassionately at the inert man.

'You've killed him,' Beth whispered in horror.

'No, I haven't. I know how hard to hit, and with him

it's not very hard. He may have an aching jaw and a few loose teeth to explain away—but he'll live.' He looked hard at Beth. 'You're a fool—and a troublemaker.'

'Thanks,' she said bitterly. 'I went for a quiet walk, that's all.'

'Then you should stay in the house and do some knitting or something.'

Her temper flared. 'You're no better than him! I don't have to do what *you* tell me——'

'Don't raise your voice to me.' His tone should have warned her, but she had had enough of both him and Ralph, and the shock was subsiding, leaving an anger in its place.

'I'll raise my voice if I want to!' she snapped. 'It's a pity I can't use my fists like you, or I'd show you——'

'Shut up!' He turned away. She grabbed his arm, the white heat of her temper focussing on him now. He shook her hand off, as if brushing away a fly, and something snapped inside her.

She pummelled his back with her clenched fists, sobbing, and he turned, caught her, held her with a grip of steel, and kissed her. Then lifted his face away, eyes darkened, and whispered: 'Is that what you want? Is it?' Then he kissed her again, the welling up anger inside him matching her own. She fought, she struggled, silently, she tried to escape the hard, demanding mouth, and of course, she knew it was precisely what she had wanted all along. But she would die before she admitted it even to herself.

At last he was finished with her, and he laughed, and tilted up her chin.

'That's what you would have got from him—and more,' he said. 'But that can wait. I'm a patient man.' The anger had nearly gone from his eyes. He looked aside at Ralph, as the other tried to stand. 'There'll be another time, another place.' He looked back at Beth, looked her up and down slowly, as if stripping her, and his face told more than his words. 'Then—then you'll know.'

A strange excitement filled her. She saw it all in his eyes, saw what was there, and her body was weak with the desire she knew he possessed—she tried to smile, but it didn't work. But he did, because he knew. He turned away, still smiling, and bent to heft the sullen Ralph to his feet.

'Come along, baby,' he said. 'Back to the house. You can leave in the morning first thing. I think we've had enough of you here. You can tell Ruth whatever you like—I don't think you'd like to tell her the truth—something on the lines of, you fell against a door, should cover everything nicely.'

Ralph had nothing to say. Not surprisingly, for he was holding his bruised jaw, testing to see if it was broken, presumably. 'No, it's not,' said Ryan, as if knowing. 'I didn't hit you hard enough to break it. I could have,' he added cheerfully, 'but I didn't want to, because it would have meant you staying here a while longer.' He looked at Beth. 'What are you waiting for? It's no use us all trooping back together. Ruth's not stupid. She'd see your face and she'd know, and I don't intend to shatter her illusions at this stage. It's straight ahead. See that oak with the twisted branch. Go past that—you'll see the house. We'll be in soon. Ralph and I have one or two things to discuss.'

Without a word, Beth left them. She ran as if pursued, saw the house, ran in through the unlocked front door, and up to her bedroom, mercifully seeing neither Ruth or her grandfather. Safely inside, she sat down on the bed, took her coat off, then tried to calm herself. She felt shattered, both mentally and physically. Too much had happened, too soon. She took off the wellingtons and felt for her slippers under the bed. The image of Ryan's face swam into her mind, making her dizzy. He was totally ruthless. He always got what he wanted. And he wanted her.

CHAPTER EIGHT

THE two men weren't at lunch. When Beth eventually went downstairs, fearful of what she might see, there was silence. No raised voices, nothing. Her grandfather sat in the lounge reading a book and greeted her cheerfully when she went in. 'Looking for Ruth?' he enquired.

'Er—yes.' She looked at him. He sat there, happily and blandly, book on knee. Nothing amiss there.

'She's in the kitchen. Did you have a nice walk?'

'Lovely, thanks,' she lied. 'I went to sit in the chapel—it's very peaceful there, isn't it?'

'Yes. It's been used for generations by our family.' He sighed. 'I've not been down for a while——'

'I'll take you if you like,' Beth offered. She had seen the wheelchair discreetly tucked away in a butler's pantry off the kitchen.

'Would you?' his face brightened. 'That'll be nice. I should see it before the wedding.'

'It needs a bit of dusting and polishing. I thought I'd go down and give it a clean—if no one minds that is.'

'Bless you! That's a good idea. You're a thoughtful girl, Beth, I like that. Ryan knew what he was doing when he married you.'

She had forgotten! She had actually forgotten that he —and only he—didn't know the truth. For a moment she was lost for words, but her grandfather didn't notice. He nodded. 'Yes, Ryan's like a son to me—which makes you one of the family.' Her heart ached. If only he knew the truth of it!

'Thank you,' she said simply, and wondered why the lump in her throat wouldn't go away. A great wave of sadness washed over her, and she wanted to cry. 'I'll go and fix it up with Ruth, then. At least I won't get lost if I'm with you.'

'Lost?' he echoed.

She smiled. 'I only found the chapel by chance. Until then I'd been wandering through the trees wondering if I'd ever see Witchwood again!'

'Ah, and there's twenty acres of them too! Poor Beth. You should have let Ryan show you round. He knows his way blindfold.' I'll bet he does, she thought wryly. It seemed a good opportunity to ask her question.

'Is there any reason for the name Witchwood?' she asked him. 'Any legend or anything like that?'

'Bless you, yes! Didn't Ryan tell you? The house is named after the woods actually. The house was built in —let me see—1805—my memory's not what it was, but we've the deeds somewhere. I must show you some time—fascinating sheet of paper, about five feet long, covered in sealing wax and signatures and that lovely old copperplate writing——' he rambled on, and Beth waited, calm and patient, knowing he was lost in the past, and with no intention of disturbing him. Then she realised he had come back from his bout of nostalgic reminiscence.

'Where was I?' he said.

'Witchwood—the legend?' she prompted.

He grinned, looked suddenly very boyish. 'Ah yes. I do wander occasionally, don't I?' He chuckled. 'You're too polite to agree—but I know I do it. Well, yes, now about 1790 it would be—we've got a book on it some-where in the library, remind me after. There was a girl living in the village nearby, and she was called——' he paused. 'Good gracious!'

'What?' Beth was alarmed at the expression on his face for a moment.

He laughed. 'Nothing wrong. Just that her name was the same as yours—Beth. Beth Linden she was too——' it was strange, hearing her own name, however innocently, from his lips. 'She would be an ancestor of mine, indirectly, probably a great-great-great aunt or similar, and she had the gift—or in those days the curse—of second sight. Nowadays she'd be considered psychic and no more would be thought of it 'cept she'd probably make money telling fortunes, but in those days, the poor child—and that's all she was, barely eighteen—she was looked at askance because she made the mistake of telling people what she could see.' He nodded and closed his eyes briefly. 'Like, for example, she told a local farmer he'd better watch his sheep, there was a snowstorm coming up and he'd be losing some—only it was spring, and no thoughts of snow in anyone's minds at all, beautiful weather—only it happened like she said, and if he'd heeded her warnings he'd have got the flock down to lower pastures, but he didn't, and lost half his stock in the blizzard a day later.' He shook his head. 'Then she saved a little boy from drowning. He'd been missing all day and she went to his mother and told her she "saw" him clinging to a rock by a stream, and led the villagers to the place, and there he was, sure enough, trapped by floodwater, and clinging on for dear life to a boulder in the middle of the river where he'd been trying to cross.'

'But surely they were grateful?' she burst out.

'Oh yes, but you see it didn't seem natural she should know. You get me? To them, and they were simple country folk, it seemed she was a witch. They looked askance at her after that. And no doubt the thoughts were in their minds—maybe she *caused* those things to happen in the first place. It must have made life difficult for her.'

Beth felt a sudden pang of sympathy for her name-sake—her ancestress too—though she could not say it. 'Where does the wood come into it?' she asked gently.

'It's where she vanished,' he answered simply, and an icy trickle of shock ran down her spine.

'Vanished?' she whispered.

'Aye. Just disappeared—and was never seen again.'

'How?' She couldn't have moved if she had tried.

'She had a sweetheart, a boy from another village. He either didn't know or didn't care about her reputation as a witch, and they used to meet in the woods—these woods—and one night she sneaked out to meet him, only she never did. He never saw her, not that night, so he went back home. The following night when she didn't turn up he went to her home—and they told him she'd gone out the night before and not returned. Perhaps they were relieved, who knows? She was one of ten children, and things had been getting very unpleasant for her family recently what with all the talk and rumours. Perhaps they thought she'd run off somewhere. The boy, her sweetheart, was heartbroken. He made them search the woods for days and days, and he used to return there every night for months afterwards and wait for her—until one day, in winter, they found him lying dead, frozen stiff——'

'Please stop,' whispered Beth.

He smiled gently. 'I know. I'm sorry. I'll stop if you want, only—well, there's a bit more, might make you feel better.'

She shuddered. 'How could it?'

'Shall I tell you?'

She nodded. The story had had the strangest effect on her. Before she had reached the chapel, at one point in her wandering, it had seemed to her she had heard faint and distant laughter. Not mocking or sinister, but the laughter of a happy child. . . .

'When they found him—so the legend goes—he had a smile on his face of pure happiness, and in his hand was a scrap of material—from the dress she had been wearing the night she'd disappeared.'

Beth looked at her grandfather, wordless, and he nodded gently. 'They say that sometimes, on a clear night, when the moon is full, they can be seen walking hand in hand through the woods.' He sat back. 'Don't look so worried, my dear. I've never seen them and I've lived here all my life.'

Strangely enough, she felt better. 'I'm not worried,' she answered, and it was the truth. 'What a fascinating story.'

'I've not told it for years,' he admitted. 'But you're right, it is. And now you know how the house got its name.'

'Thank you for telling me.' She stood up. 'I'd better go and help Ruth.' She had completely forgotten the morning's unpleasantness, and it was with surprise that she heard Ruth say, minutes later:

'Ryan's taken Ralph to the dentist in Buxton—a filling came out of one of his teeth.'

Beth stood in the kitchen doorway, her mind a blank. Teeth—dentist—filling? She was wrenched back from the Witchwood legend with a bump. 'Good heavens,' she said, because it was all she could say. At least, she remembered now.

'So we won't wait lunch. It's only fish anyway, I can do theirs later.'

'Yes. Yes, of course.' She wondered what explanation —official explanation—had been made for the loss of a filling. She hardly dared to ask, because she couldn't trust herself to sound natural. Ruth, however, busily warming plates, began to explain.

'There you are, love, just pull up a chair, we'll eat out here—that's it—Ralph had gone off out to find you, and set off back when he didn't see you—I dare say you'd come back another way—and he fell and ricked his ankle on a rabbit hole—came down heavily, poor boy, and nearly knocked himself out, fortunately Ryan heard him shout out and came back with him. Dear me,' she smiled at Beth, 'those woods aren't safe, are they? Good job you didn't get lost as well!'

Beth laughed. 'No—well, I *nearly* did,' she amended. 'Then I found the chapel. That's a good landmark. I'm taking Adam down there for a walk—if that's all right?'

'Do him good. Lovely.'

It seemed safe to ask a question now that the first explanations were over. 'I hope Ralph's not hurt himself— I mean, with his new job?'

'No. He's got a bruise on his chin, but it'll fade in a day or two. He did say he wanted to leave tomorrow. He's got a pal in London who'll lend him a flat for a week or two until he finds somewhere, and he wants to get down there as soon as possible before anyone else turns up.'

'Oh yes, I know how it is,' agreed Beth, hating herself for the deception she too was involved in. She wondered what Ryan had said to Ralph after she had left them. A lot in a few words, she decided. Whatever it was, it had worked. And now they'd gone out together in a car, and would presumably return together soon enough, and she would take it from there. She felt exhausted, mentally and physically. She hoped they would be gone a while. Preferably a year or two....

But they returned when she was walking back to the house pushing her grandfather in his wheelchair after walking round the chapel with him.

She heard the car's engine, and moved to one side of the drive and waited for it to pass. Instead it stopped, Ryan got out, and Ralph drove on.

'I'll push that,' said Ryan. She stood aside, her grandfather craned to see him, and chuckled.

'Spoilsport,' he grumbled. 'We were having a nice chat.'

Ryan laughed, including Beth in his laughter. 'Sorry about that,' he said. 'Why do you think I broke it up? I know you too well, you old devil.'

Beth concentrated on walking demurely by the side of the chair, leaving them to their banter. Ryan was the bland, charming man who never said a word out of place when her grandfather was there, and she needed the break. The house came into sight, Ryan's car at the front, and she asked innocently: 'Did everything go all right at the dentist?'

'Perfectly,' he assured her. 'Ralph had loosened a couple of teeth when he fell, but everything's fine now.'

'Oh, good.' She smiled down at her grandfather. 'Adam's been telling me the story of Witchwood—I don't think I'll go wandering there alone again either.'

'No,' answered Ryan drily. 'I'll take you when you want to go.'

'I don't want you vanishing,' said Adam. 'No wandering down there after dark, you hear me?'

Beth laughed in genuine amusement. The idea of going anywhere with Ryan alone once night had fallen was almost too funny for words. 'Don't worry,' she said, and gave Ryan a gentle, loving look for the benefit of her grandfather. 'Though Ryan would take care of me, wouldn't you, darling?'

'I'd do my best,' he answered. The look he gave her couldn't be seen by the old man, because Ryan was directly behind him, but it was as potent as words. It said—just you wait, oh, just you wait!

She wondered then how long the shabby deception must go on. She felt like a traitor. She felt—dirty. And at that moment she hated herself most of all.

It was as if Ryan knew, for he changed the subject by telling Adam of someone they had seen at the dentist, who knew him and had asked after him, and sent his regards. Then they were nearing the back of the house, where it was easier to manoeuvre the chair in, because there was only one step, and Beth's bad moment passed.

It returned later when, while she was alone in the library looking for the book about the legend, Ryan came in and closed the door after him. She turned round. 'Please go away,' she said.

'I've come to use the telephone. I didn't know you were here,' he answered.

'Then I'll go. I was only looking for a book. I'll do it afterwards.' She had no fight left in her, and she knew she could not cope with him if she sparked his usual aggression. All she wanted was to be left in peace. She walked towards the door.

'I can wait. Find your book,' he said.

'It doesn't matter. There's no hurry.' He had made no attempt to move away from the door, and she looked at him in silent appeal. 'Please,' she said.

Something filled the room—a deep, throbbing tension, older than time. She felt as if she had been standing there for ever, waiting for him to move, and she had no strength, none at all, and her face was white. Ryan looked down at her, and he seemed larger than life, a tall powerful man, taking all her strength—or what little she now possessed—from her, just by looking at her. And the moment stretched, and became timeless itself, and she thought she would faint. She closed her eyes, felt herself sway, then his arms were upon hers, steadying her ever so gently.

'You're not well,' he said. Was that concern in his voice? It was something she had never heard before, from him.

'I'm all right,' she answered, and the words seemed to come from far away, as if she too heard them, yet had not spoken them. 'Please—let me free.' She had meant to say 'let me go' yet she had said 'free', and she didn't know why. She felt her legs give beneath her, and would have fallen, but he picked her up in his arms and carried her out of the room and up the stairs. There was no one about. Ruth and her grandfather were watching television, Ralph was out. Ryan walked along to her room, opened the door and carried her in. He laid her on the bed, then went to close the door. Then he returned and sat by her side.

'I'll get you a drink of water,' he said, and went into the bathroom. She heard the tap running, then he brought out a glass of water and lifted her head slightly. 'Drink,' he said.

Beth sipped the water and pushed his hand away. 'You would have fainted,' he said.

'No.' She stared up at him. It was dark in the room, and only the light from the bathroom traced a pattern across the carpet, not reaching the bed. The room was shadow-filled, and she was afraid of him, afraid to be alone with him, yet she dared not say.

'Yes,' he said softly. 'Is it because of what happened today? He is going tomorrow.'

Doesn't he know? she thought. Doesn't he know I can deal with the Ralphs of this world? It's the Ryans I can't deal with. Only there was only one Ryan; he wasn't a type, like Ralph.

'No,' she said. 'It's not that.' She shook her head. 'Why don't you go?'

'I can't leave you like this.'

'Yes, you can. Quite easily. You only have to get up and walk out.' She closed her eyes. She didn't want him to touch her—yet she wanted him to kiss her. It was too much of a contradiction for her to cope with.

Then his hand was on her forehead, the pressure gentle, cooling her. 'Don't tell me I've got a temperature,' she whispered, in a vain attempt at humour.

'I doubt it.' But he didn't remove his hand, and she didn't attempt to move her head.

There was an ache in her throat, an ache from tears suppressed. 'Why don't you——' she had to clear her throat, 'go down and make your telephone call?'

'It can wait.'

'I'll go to bed, if that makes you feel easier about me. You can tell Ruth I have a headache—tell her anything.'

'Very well.' The gentle pressure was removed, and the weight from her bed, and he stood looking down at her. Then he was gone.

Beth was left alone, and lonely. She heard his footsteps recede, then she got up, went into the bathroom and washed and undressed. She didn't feel well, she felt wretched in fact, and she knew an early night would help. She lay dozing, half asleep, half awake, and images of the day came back to her, and she moved restlessly, not knowing the time, not caring, wanting only to be alone—and yet not alone. And when later the tap came at the door she knew who it was.

Beth woke up before dawn, and lay there, warm and comfortable in her bed, surfacing gradually from the mists of the dreams, and as the dreams receded, memory returned. With the memories came a warmth, and then, softly, she began to weep.

She didn't want to stay any longer at Witchwood, but she had no choice. The wedding would take place within two weeks, and after that, what then? Ruth had virtually offered her a home for as long as she cared to stay. Ruth, who knew the true reason for her visit. But her grandfather didn't. He thought she was there because she was Ryan's wife, and that they were on their honeymoon—and that they were looking forward to his wedding. If she walked out now it would not merely upset him, it could be disastrous to his health. Whatever happened, Beth could not have anything like that on her conscience. She was trapped—in a web of her own making. The web she had started spinning at the moment she had agreed to go to Witchwood as Ryan's wife.

She lay and stared at the ceiling, not really seeing anything except that which was in her mind. Ryan had come in with a cup of tea, and the book for which she had been searching previously, on the legend of Witchwood.

'I've brought the book you were looking for,' he had told her. 'Ruth found it for me, and a cup of tea. She wants to know if you need anything else?'

'Nothing, thanks.' She had turned her head away, willing him to leave.

'Do you want the light on?'

'No.'

He sat down on the bed, and she felt the weight, and moved her legs slightly away. 'Is it because I hit Ralph?' he asked softly.

'It's nothing to do with that. It's nothing to do with you,' she answered equally softly. 'Go away.' She had kept her face averted, and suddenly he took hold of her chin and turned her to face him. She heard his sharply indrawn breath when he saw the tears glistening in her eyes, but she made no effort to blink them away.

'Then what is it? Tell me.'

'If you don't know, I couldn't even begin——' she stopped, her voice dangerously shaky. There was a silence. A silence which grew, stretched, tautened— then he muttered, in a voice she could scarcely hear:

'Oh, my God!' There was anguish and despair there in those three words. She turned, lifted her hand to touch his face, and she didn't know why she did it, except that there was a need. Ryan said no more; he kissed her. It was a kiss of infinite tenderness.... And she remembered the moments in the library, when time had stood still, and it was happening again, and in it she sensed his hidden despair, and she didn't know why, but it didn't matter any more.

Then he was gone, a dark shadow leaving the room. She was alone, and she slept. Her sleep was dream-filled, wild tempestuous dreams of running through an endless forest of trees, knowing no escape, no way out—the dreams changed, the quality was finer. She was still lost, but it was no longer important, for she knew she would find what she was seeking.

Now awake, dreams fading to shreds of forgetfulness, she watched the sun come up outside the window and gradually lighten the room. Beth felt very calm now, calm and cool and different. She breathed deeply and slowly, and knew something in her life had changed irrevocably. And now, and until she left Witchwood, she would devote her time to the grandfather she had found so late, and whether he ever knew the truth about the relationship was no longer a major issue. She loved him dearly, she had come to know that over the days she had been there, and the rights and wrongs of what happened years ago with her father and uncle were gone and finished.

Slowly she got out of bed and went to have a bath, and wash her hair.

She was able to wish Ralph farewell in a perfectly normal manner. He left after lunch to travel down to London, and they all stood at the front door to wave him off, and Ruth wiped away a tear as they went back into the hall. Beth put her arm round the older woman's shoulder as Ryan closed the front door. 'Let's go and have a cup of tea,' she said.

'A good idea.' Ruth smiled at her. They went into the kitchen, leaving Adam and Ryan to make their way into the lounge, there to continue an endless chess game. In the kitchen it was warm and cosy, with a roaring fire leaping up the chimney. They sat and toasted their toes by it as they drank their tea. 'We'll have to take the two men a cup in a few minutes, I suppose,' said Ruth. 'But it's nice just to sit here for a while and chat.'

'It is,' Beth smiled. 'Have you everything ready for the wedding?'

'I want to buy a suit—will you come shopping with me?'

'Love to.'

'Apart from that everything's arranged. It will be a very simple quiet ceremony, as you know. Just you and Ryan as witnesses, and of course if Ralph can manage——' Ruth's voice tailed off wistfully.

'Let's hope so,' agreed Beth, with an enthusiasm she didn't feel. 'And then what? Back here for a meal?'

'Yes, with the vicar, of course. The woman who cleans for us will have everything ready here. Then that's it.'

'And you'll be Mrs Linden—and my grandmother.' Which will make Ralph a sort of step-uncle, she added to herself with faint dismay.

'Yes. Will you stay, Beth? Will you?'

It was an unexpected question, yet not entirely so. And Beth had to be honest. 'I want to spend a lot of time here with you,' she answered, 'but——'

'I know, love. You've got your own life to lead— heavens, it's very quiet here, I know that—but as much as you can spare. After all, as you said yourself, London's not far, not with all these motorways——'

'No, it isn't.' She laughed. 'Except I'll think twice about driving up when there's any snow likely——' and when there's any chance of Ryan being here, she added to herself.

'Oh yes. What a coincidence, though, you should meet Ryan like that.'

'Wasn't it just?' There must have been something Beth couldn't hide in her tone, for Ruth gave her an odd little look.

'Something's happened,' she said quietly. It wasn't even a question.

'Yes, something's happened. I must get away from him—for my own peace of mind. Oh, never fear, it'll be all sweetness and light while we're here. I wouldn't hurt Adam for the world—but when we leave, I shan't see him again.'

'But—Adam thinks——'

'I know. He thinks we're man and wife.' Beth put her hand over her eyes to hide the pain for an instant. 'But it'll work out. He'll have you—we'll think of something for the future.' She had to change the subject before her new-found calm disintegrated. 'When we go shopping I'll buy an outfit for the wedding as well. And of course, a present. Do you have a list?'

'Heavens, no!' Ruth chuckled. 'But it's nice of you to ask. We'll have a look round the shops—it'll be fun.' She stood up. 'Well, I'd better make their tea, then Adam can go for a rest.'

'And I think I'll make a start on cleaning the chapel.' Beth stood up as well. 'Just lead me to the buckets and mops—oh! What about water? Is there any there?'

'Only a cold tap in the vestry. Oh dear!' Ruth looked in comic dismay at Beth, who laughed.

'Don't *worry*. I'll manage.'

'Ah, wait. We've got several of those large plastic containers—I'll fill them up with hot water and Ryan can take them——'

'I can take them——' began Beth.

'Indeed you can't! You're not lugging those heavy things full of hot water around. Ryan will take them in the car.' Ruth put the kettle on and bustled out of the kitchen. Her voice came faintly from the washroom off it. 'Here we are, come and help me carry these, Beth——'

Beth followed, and the next few minutes were spent carrying all the necessary cleaning materials back into the kitchen. Then Ruth made the tea and took it in to the men, and Beth began filling the plastic containers from the hot tap.

When she had finished, Ryan came into the kitchen. He looked at her. 'I'm going down with those in the car,' he said. 'Anything else you want taking?'

'Yes.' She indicated the two buckets packed with cloths and cleaning powder. 'And this squeezy mop.'

'Right.' He nodded, opened the back door, and began to carry them out. Beth went up to change into her jeans and warm red sweater. She felt icy cold.

She walked down to the chapel, and his car was on the drive, the back door open. She looked in. He had taken everything into the chapel. She closed his door and walked away from his car towards the chapel where, two days previously, she had had the unpleasant encounter with Ralph. There would be no repetition of that with Ryan! She intended to thank him for carrying the water down, then get on with what she had come to do. Everything was neatly lined up inside the door. Of Ryan there was no sign. Beth emptied hot water into one of the buckets, added the cleaning powder, picked up a cloth, and began work. She had made her plans beforehand. The wood needed a good clean before any attempt at polishing could be made, and this she was going to do first. The floor would come later. She heard a car start up outside and move away, and thought wryly that he must have been hiding, waiting for her to go. She really didn't care.

Time passed, and there was a satisfaction in seeing the dirt disappear, and refilling the bucket with fresh water to begin again in another section, and Beth was hot with her exertions, but enjoying what she was doing. She had put a plaster over her cut hand, and a rubber glove over that to protect it, and after a particularly difficult corner pew was cleaned she stood back and wiped her forehead.

'Phew!' she surveyed what she had done, and smiled at herself. 'That looks better.'

Then Ryan walked in, and she was no longer warm, she was icy cold. She knew why; he was like a remote, glacial, stranger. 'I've brought you a flask of coffee,' he said.

She turned and looked at him coolly. 'Thank you. You can put it down at the back. I'll have it in a minute.' She turned away and recommenced rubbing vigorously on a wooden seat.

'Do you need any help?'

'I prefer to work alone.' She didn't look up. Her tone was dismissive enough on its own.

'There's too much for you to do alone.'

'Then I'll just keep on every day until it's done.' She turned to look at him then. 'The less I see of you the better.' Her eyes said it all for her. The atmosphere was charged, and she saw his face change, harden. A muscle moved in his jaw, and he had never looked so formidable, so—frightening. Beth lifted her chin. 'Go away,' she said very quietly. 'I hate you.'

She thought for a moment that he would strike her. Never had she seen such anger on a man's face. The very floor seemed to vibrate. Then he turned and walked out.

Beth sat down, her legs trembling. She never wanted to see that look on his face again. She put her hand to her mouth. 'Dear God, what have I done?' she whispered. She looked around her. It seemed she was in a strange, alien place, very cold and shadowed, and her own words echoed mockingly in her ears—I hate you—I hate you—

But she didn't hate him at all.

CHAPTER NINE

SHE worked in the chapel until she was nearly dropping with exhaustion. She had no idea of time; her watch had stopped. The coffee had been finished long before, and she had found the light switch when it grew darker and turned on all the lamps, which cast a soft warming glow round the chapel. She was completely alone, and glad to be so. But she couldn't stay there all night. She stood back and surveyed what she had done, stretched, and rubbed her hand along her aching back. 'Ouch!' It was no use; she was too tired to do more. But tomorrow....

She opened the door, letting in cold air, looked out, and shivered. Then she emptied the bucket, picked up the empty flask, after putting on her coat, switched out the lights and closed the door behind her. She stood in the porch looking out at the blackness surrounding her, and all she had to do was to walk to the drive. And she couldn't move. It was ridiculous, absurd—and she didn't believe in ghosts or anything supernatural, but——

Ryan. She thought his name, but he wouldn't come to fetch her. She had effectively dismissed him hours before, and he would be playing one of his interminable games of chess with her grandfather by a bright fire in a warm lighted room, and if he thought of her at all it would be with contempt. And Ruth rarely ventured out after dark, as she had told Beth cheerfully, because she could never see a darned thing and always managed to trip over something....

So what do I do? thought Beth. Stand here shaking like a leaf all night? The wind soughed gently through the trees, and they stirred and shivered slightly, the leafless branches stark against the fainter lightness of the star-dotted sky, and Beth was filled with a blind panic. She turned, opened the door and almost fell into the chapel. This is *ridiculous*, she told herself firmly. But she wished, all the same, that her grandfather hadn't told her the legend. Not yet. Not until she had finished cleaning the chapel. If she set off, walking *very quickly*, not looking *anywhere* except straight ahead, it would be only—well, a hundred and fifty steps to the drive. That was all. She could count them. And now was the time to go, before she had too much time to brood about things. *Things*. Shadows and strange moving shapes——— 'Stop it!' she said out aloud, marched to the door, opened it and went out.

One—two—three—four—oh, for a torch!—five—six —seven—and a huge black shape loomed out of the trees ahead of her, and Beth screamed.

'For God's sake———' Ryan caught her as she turned in blind panic to flee, and she collapsed into his arms.

'Oh! Oh!' she gulped. 'I—I———'

'Don't try to talk.' He held her arm now, began walking towards the drive with her. 'Don't *explain*. I know.'

Her terror had vanished now. She was safe. At least, safe from the dark shadows, and that, at the moment, was all that mattered. She took a deep shuddery breath.

'I heard you call me,' he said. 'I knew.'

'*What?*' What on earth was he talking about? They were nearing the drive now, and the trees thinned, and there had been no ghosts at all, just her vivid imagination at work, but she didn't understand what he was saying, except that it didn't make any kind of sense.

He stopped and looked down at her. 'I don't know.' She saw a frown on his blurred shadowy face. 'I heard you call me—but I couldn't have done.'

'No,' she said flatly. 'Why would I call *you*?'

'Because you were terrified of walking home in the dark.'

They reached the drive. They began to walk towards the house, side by side, only a foot or so between them physically, but a world apart. At least Beth owed him some explanation of her blind terror, and she couldn't bear the silence which was growing. 'I was,' she admitted, 'but my grandfather had told me the story of the girl in the wood yesterday, and——'

'I know that. He said so.'

'That's all. I set off to come back—only I couldn't. So I went back inside and sat a moment and realised I couldn't stay there all night. Stupid—but when I saw you——' she tried a little laugh, which didn't quite come off.

'Logical. I didn't frighten you deliberately.'

'I know.' They could see the house now, lit up as if in welcome, waiting for them. 'But how could you think you heard me?'

Ryan shrugged. 'Does it matter?'

'No,' she said very quietly. But it did, because in her fear she had thought strongly about him, had thought his name. And while she didn't believe in ghosts, she did believe in telepathy. But then that only happened between people who were close, who could pick up each other's thoughts because they loved one another. . . . 'No,' she said again, as if in silent protest against something.

And he looked at her. And perhaps he knew. She didn't want to talk about it any more. 'I forgot the flask,' she said.

'That doesn't matter either. It'll do tomorrow.'

'Yes.'

As they went up the steps she said: 'Thank you for coming for me.'

'Am I supposed to reply—it was a pleasure? Because I don't intend to.'

'You don't have to reply at all.' As they went in, she looked at him. 'But I had to say it, because I was scared.'

'You shouldn't have stayed there so long. You don't get overtime for working after dark.' He closed the door, shutting out the cold night air.

'No. But I have my reasons.'

'And I can guess what they are. Or rather, I don't need to guess, do I? I already know.' He smiled thinly, and his eyes were dark shadows.

'Yes, you do.' Beth turned and walked away from him. She went up to her room to wash and change, then went and found Ruth in the kitchen preparing dinner.

'Just in time,' she said. 'My, you look as though you've been working hard! Did Ryan meet you?'

'Yes. I was just plucking up my courage—I shouldn't have stayed after dark, Ruth, but I lost count of time, and I scared myself thinking of that poor girl——'

'I can guess. You poor thing! Here, have a drop of sherry, you deserve it.' She handed Beth a glass and indicated the bottle. 'Just help yourself. It was funny, that, with Ryan.'

Beth sat, wincing as her aching muscles protested. 'Funny? What was?'

'The way he jumped up as if he'd been shot, and said —"That's odd—did you hear it?" And I looked at Adam, and Adam looked at me, and we both said "Hear what?" together. And he said "I heard Beth shout to me." ' She looked at Beth, a smile lighting her eyes. 'Then he went out, leaving Adam and me gaping.'

'Oh,' said Beth. She sipped the sherry. She did need a drink. 'I certainly didn't shout to anyone. The chapel's too far away from the house anyway.'

'True. I thought you must have come back, you see. When he'd been gone ten minutes I realised you hadn't. Well, never mind, dinner's ready now. Let's take it in, shall we?' And the subject was closed. But not forgotten. It returned to tease Beth as she lay in bed later that night, too wide awake to sleep. It was eerie, and she didn't understand it, and thought she never would. She turned to watch the moon through the window, streaming in, casting pale yellow light where it spilled across the carpet, making the shadows darker in contrast. It was nearly midnight. The following day she and Ruth were going in Adam's car shopping while Ryan stayed with Adam. Beth had spent the evening going over old family papers with her grandfather. There had been the ideal excuse. She had wanted to see the deeds of the house, which had involved boxes of papers being found—and loads of old photographs. She had enjoyed the evening, nostalgia mingling with her affection for the old man. And at one point, when she was alone with him, Ryan and Ruth having left to make supper, he had picked up a faded wedding photograph and handed it to Beth. She sensed now—in retrospect—that he had waited deliberately until they were alone, but that thought had not struck her then. 'See that,' he had said. 'Guess who?'

It was easy. Beth had laughed. 'It's you,' she answered.

'Yes.' He had taken the photograph back and looked at it fondly. 'And soon I'm getting married again. I'm a lucky man, Beth.'

'I know you are,' she said softly.

'She looks like you,' he said.

'Ruth?' Beth smiled. She couldn't really see——

'No. Elizabeth, my first wife.' Beth's heart had begun to bump. He was talking about her grandmother.

'Oh, let me see.' She took the photograph back and studied it. Her own eyes looked back at her from the young woman by the very young Adam's side. The likeness cried out.

'I thought it when you first came,' he mused quietly, 'but I said nothing. But you're very like her.'

'She was very beautiful——' she paused, realising what she had said. 'Oh! I didn't mean that I'm——'

'I know.' He laughed. 'I know what you mean. But you *are* beautiful, you know, my dear.' He had looked at her, and if that had been the moment she would have told him, because it seemed almost as if he knew. But she dared not. Then the others had returned, and the moment had gone. Now, looking back over the evening, Beth wondered at the spark in Adam's eyes when he had spoken to her. Almost as if he had been waiting for confirmation of something in his mind. She sighed, and turned away from the moonlight. What a strange, tangled world I live in, she thought. And it all seemed so simple and straightforward only weeks ago, when I discovered that I had a grandfather. And now I'm here, with him, but not in the way I imagined.

She sat up. She was more wide awake than when she had come to bed, and her arms, legs, and back hurt with the not unpleasant ache of sheer hard physical work. The house was silent. Everyone was in bed, even Ryan. If she crept down to the kitchen and made herself a drink of tea, no one would hear. And if there was any liniment in the first aid box she would bring that back too. She pulled her dressing gown on, belted it tightly, and crept to the door, listening for a moment before opening it. Then she went very quietly along the corridor, holding her breath as she passed Ryan's room, from under whose door a thin sliver of light showed.

Safely in the kitchen she put on the kettle and found the first aid box. There was no liniment, but there was a tube of cream which was not only for rheumatic pains, but apparently ideal for muscular aches and strains. That would do. She put it on the table and found a beaker. The fire had died down to a warm glow. She decided to drink her tea by it, then return to bed. She made the tea, found a newspaper, and sat down. It was peaceful in the kitchen, with only the slow ticking of the clock breaking the silence of the night. Then, from somewhere overhead, a board creaked, and her scalp prickled. The sound wasn't repeated, and she forgot about it as she read the latest depressing news about the economy, and began to yawn with the sheer boredom of it all.

The door opened and she looked up. 'Oh. It's you,' he said flatly.

'Yes, it's me. Do you *mind*?' She glared at Ryan, who stood there in dressing gown, barefooted. 'Do you have to follow me about?' His tone had stung her into anger, though she couldn't have said why.

'I heard a noise from down here.'

'And now you know who it was,' she retorted. 'I'm not a burglar. I'm having a cup of tea—and I'm quite sure Ruth won't mind.'

He came forward and picked up the tube of cream. 'Is this yours?'

'No,' she answered sweetly. 'It belongs to the house. Only I'm borrowing it.'

'You shouldn't have worked so hard. I warned you——'

'Oh, shut up, do!' She closed the newspaper and flung it aside. 'I don't need you to look after me! Or were you going to suggest rubbing it on for me? I've heard that one before.'

'No, I wasn't.' He stood looking down at her, and she couldn't stand it any longer. She walked over to the sink and rinsed her cup.

'If you're staying, I'm going,' she said. 'Goodnight.' At the door she paused, turned, stared at him. 'I'm securing my door,' she said.

'Did you think I would try and break in?' He looked almost amused.

'Nothing would surprise me with you,' she answered bitterly.

'Then in that case you would do well to barricade your door.' His voice was soft. 'You may sleep better. Who knows?' He shrugged. He looked her up and down. 'You didn't throw me out when——'

She whirled away and slammed the door behind her, regretting it instantly lest she woke Ruth or her grandfather. Furious, humiliated, she stalked down the corridor, heard the door open after her, heard his voice: 'Wait!'

It held all the authority in the world. She swung round angrily and he came up to her holding the tube of cream.

'It's easier to make a grand exit when you remember to take everything,' he remarked.

She snatched it from him, the shadows of the passage hiding her angry, scarlet cheeks. Ryan laughed, as if he knew, and incensed, Beth struck out at him. 'Smile about *that*!' she breathed, as her hand connected with his mocking face.

He caught her arm, still uplifted, and pulled her roughly to him. 'All right,' he whispered, 'I will.' She saw the gleam of his teeth, shadowed, but clear enough. 'Do you think you can hurt me?' The grip of his fingers tightened on her wrist. 'You've no more strength than a child——'

'Let me *go*!'

'When you say—"I shouldn't have hit you, Ryan." '

'Get lost!'

The fingers tightened like a vice. 'Now,' he said softly.

'You bully—you——'

'Yes, I know, and more. Say it, then.'

'No, I won't! You can——'

He caught hold of her other arm. The ointment fell to the ground. She was completely powerless. Her heart thudded against her ribs in sudden fear. She couldn't scream, or shout for help—and she couldn't escape. And the contest was suddenly a battle of wills—but she knew she must not give in, or she was lost. 'Beat me,' she whispered scornfully, 'if that's what you want. But you won't make me say——'

'Yes, I will.' He kissed her, fiercely and savagely. 'Because if you don't I'll make love to you here and now——'

He meant it too. A wild excitement filled her body as he pressed her against the wall, all his weight against her, and began to kiss her in a way that left no doubt of his intentions. 'No,' she protested, and the sound was drowned by his lips, seeking, demanding, punishing——

She tried to move but was helpless. She tried to push him, but she might as well have tried to push an irresistible force. Confused, nearly lost, she found the will to say: 'Not here——' she added, 'Wait——' and felt him move slightly away.

It was her chance—the only one she would get, she knew. She wriggled free and ran as fast as she could, as if pursued by a thousand ghosts—and only when she was half way up the stairs in a headlong flight did she realise Ryan had made no attempt to follow her. She collapsed in her room, pushed the small dresser against the door, and fell on to the bed. She was gasping for breath, dizzy with what had happened. But she was free. She looked in apprehension at the door. For how long? The minutes ticked past, and still no sound, and when some minutes after that she crawled into bed exhausted, she realised two things. All her aches and pains had gone —but the other was not so reassuring. She suddenly realised she hadn't really wanted to escape after all. . . .

When she awoke it was morning. The dresser was still in place, the house was silent. She looked at her watch : ten past seven. Today she was going shopping with Ruth. She remembered again the photograph she had seen of her late grandmother, another Elizabeth, and as she did so she tried to recall what it was she had seen in her grandfather's eyes as he had handed the photograph to her. A waiting, a watching—perhaps no more. Perhaps he wasn't even aware of it himself. She sighed, decided it was time to get out of bed, and start preparing breakfast.

The roads were clear now, with only patches of banked-up snow, as yet unmelted, at the sides to remind them of what had been. The hills were still white blurs against the sky, which was clear and pale blue. And the sun shone. Ruth's happy mood infected Beth, and after they had parked Adam's car they found a café and went in for coffee and a cake. Beth watched the people passing out-

side, and stirred her coffee. 'Lost in thought?' Ruth
enquired gently.

'Oh! Sorry.' Beth smiled. 'Perhaps I was. I was remembering something Adam said last night——' and
she told the older woman about the photograph. Ruth
nodded thoughtfully when she had finished.

'I've wondered myself,' she admitted. 'He's never said
anything—yet I've had the feeling, when I've seen him
look at you sometimes, as if he——' she hesitated. 'I
don't know. It's difficult to put into words. It's—as
though—he's waiting for someone to tell him something.'

'But we mustn't. Not yet——'

'If he knows. If he guesses, then I don't see why not.'

Beth's heart bumped in sudden surprise. 'But—his
health——' she began.

'I know—no excitement. Leave it with me. If the
moment comes, we'll know.'

Beth impulsively clasped the other woman's hands.
'You're so wonderful,' she said, moved deeply. 'Some
women might have resented——'

'Oh, tush! Resented indeed! I'm delighted!'

'It's all been such a mix-up,' Beth said. 'I mean, me
arriving like that with Ryan——'

'But it will all work out right in the end, you'll see.'

'I wish I had your confidence,' sighed Beth.

'Oh, my dear, I always believe in looking on the
bright side.' And Ruth beamed at her. 'Now, finish your
coffee and we'll go on our little shopping expedition. Do
you know, I feel quite excited.'

'I promise you,' said Beth, 'that you'll be a real knock-
out on your wedding day. And if we don't find anything
nice enough here, I'll take you into Manchester to the
shops there. Adam won't mind his car being used——'

'But it's too far!'

'I've looked on my map. We'd be there in half an hour. So think about it. If you don't see what you want, off we go.'

Ruth giggled like a schoolgirl. 'I'll leave it to you,' she answered. 'You're the driver.'

'That's right,' agreed Beth calmly. She finished her coffee and they both went out into the crisp cold autumn day.

But there was no need to leave Buxton. At the second shop they entered, it was there. It wasn't a suit, as Ruth had decided she needed, it was a dress and matching coat in a delicious oyster shade of wild silk. As soon as Beth saw it, she knew. There were a few preliminaries to go through first, of trying on various suits, then Beth signalled the sales assistant and whispered something to her.

She ignored Ruth's feeble protests that she really needed a suit, and minutes later she emerged from the changing room in the dress and coat, and Beth nodded, well satisfied.

'Oh yes,' she said. 'Oh *yes*—you look absolutely beautiful.'

Ruth preened herself, glancing in the long mirror. 'Well——'

The sales assistant produced a nosegay of violets made in velvet, yet looking so realistic that Beth was tempted to sniff them, and pinned them to the top of the coat. 'There, madam,' she murmured. 'Now look.'

Ruth was silenced. Somehow, the violets added that touch of perfection that could not be denied. 'Oh yes,' she whispered, and smiled at herself in the mirror, 'oh dear me, yes!'

Beth and the girl looked at each other and exchanged satisfied smiles.

'Handbags?' murmured Beth. The girl nodded and vanished, and Ruth looked at the price tag on her outfit and winced.

'Shush,' said Beth, before she could even begin to say anything. 'You know you look terrific. And if you dare say anything, I'll buy the dress and coat myself!'

'I believe you would too,' laughed Ruth. 'You're quite right, it might have been made for me. Of course I'll take it. It's just my natural Derbyshire caution asserting itself.'

'Then tell it to go away. We'll get you a handbag, and buy your shoes. Then it's my turn.'

It was several hours later when they returned to Witchwood, loaded up with mysterious boxes and packages which were whisked away safely to be hidden until the big day. It was as they were in Ruth's room putting everything tidily away that Ruth brought up a subject they had discussed on the way back.

'But I'm sure that Ryan *needs* help with his papers,' she said. 'He's busy writing every night, he told me.'

'We'd discussed me doing some typing for him when we were snowbound at the cottage,' Beth answered. 'But things have changed since then,' she added bitterly.

'I know,' said Ruth quietly, 'but I just thought——' she shrugged, 'oh, I don't know—it seemed it might be an interest for you while you're here.'

'It would. Don't think,' Beth added hastily, 'that I'm bored! I'm loving every minute I spend with you and Adam—but sometimes, when it's later on at night, I could do with something to occupy my brain.'

'And of course, you know he won't ask you——'

'Nor will I offer.'

'No.' Ruth smiled softly. 'So it's up to me, isn't it?'

Beth drew in her breath sharply. 'What would you—how——' she began.

'Very *tactfully*,' answered Ruth, with unusual crispness, and nodded. 'You'll see.' Beth smiled, amused at the other's suddenly decisive manner.

They went down to a late lunch, then Beth decided she could spend a couple of hours at the chapel before it went dark. They hadn't seen Ryan at all since returning and she had no wish to, so she filled the remaining containers herself with hot water and drove down in Adam's car, leaving Ruth to prepare the evening meal.

She managed to put Ryan almost completely out of her mind as she worked busily away cleaning the floor, after finishing the pews, and keeping a careful eye on the light outside. As soon as dusk fell she would go. All was quiet. Already the chapel was a cleaner, brighter place, and Beth had a feeling of satisfaction at what she was doing. Tomorrow, she would clean the windows and polish round. . . .

There was a small sound, as of the scattering of dry leaves, a small prickle making sound. Beth felt the hairs tingle at the back of her neck, and stood very still waiting for it to come again. . . . It did, and it was from the vestry. There was an outer door there, but she had seen that it was bolted. Beth caught her breath, and stood very still. The noise came again, but now different, yet she could not have said in what way. It was sharper, more clear. She swallowed and ran her tongue along suddenly dry lips. She knew what she had to do. She would despise herself if she turned tail and fled. She had run last night, had been terrified. And there was a time to stop running, a time to face up to what you feared, and challenge it. Beth picked up the squeezy mop and marched determinedly towards the vestry door. It might not be much of a weapon against ghosts, but at least it made her feel better. . . .

She flung open the door and stepped in, ready to face she knew not what—there was a sudden clatter as a book fell from table to floor, and a bright-eyed, be-whiskered mouse bolted in terror to the safety of a mousehole in the outer wall. Beth collapsed on to a chair, her legs weak with relief. Then she began to laugh, softly at first, then louder, until the tears poured down her cheeks in the sudden release from fear. A mouse. A *mouse*! And twice as frightened as she, to judge by the speed with which it had moved. Her handbag was on the table; by its side, a bar of chocolate she had bought in Buxton. The outer wrapper had been nibbled away and a corner of the chocolate too. She picked up the bar and looked at it. Then she removed the wrapper, broke off a piece and pushed it up to the mousehole.

'Sorry, mouse,' she murmured. 'You come back for that when I'm gone.' Still chuckling, she went back to finish her cleaning.

She was telling them about it over dinner, and it amused Adam greatly. 'You're a girl after my own heart, Beth,' he told her. 'I was a great one for rescuing frogs and mice and hedgehogs when I was a lad, and bringing them home—and terrifying my mother out of her wits.' He laughed, then Ruth joined in with some anecdote of her own, while Beth listened—and watched Ryan. He was very quiet. She wondered if it was obvious to Adam. If so, he had made no comment. The dinner continued in light vein, and it no longer seemed to matter about Ryan. Ruth could talk enough for all four of them if she chose, and was now telling them of the shopping trip that had turned out so surprisingly well. Beth passed Ryan the salt as he reached out for it, and for an unavoidable second their hands touched.

'Thanks,' he said. And she saw what was in his eyes, and caught her breath. There was a deep, dark pain there. She was suddenly uneasy, and moved, seeing Adam and Ruth's empty plates. 'I'll take these out,' she offered.

'The sweet's on the fridge, dear,' Ruth said.

'None for me, thanks,' said Ryan, and pushed away his half empty plate.

'Why, Ryan, what is it?'

He smiled. 'Nothing wrong with your delicious dinner, I assure you. I'm not very hungry tonight.' Across the table Ruth's eyes met Beth's, and Beth stood up and collected the plates together, and went out. There was an uneasiness growing within her, causing her heart to beat rapidly. Was Ryan ill? He didn't look well, and the look in his eyes she found disturbing. She carried in three sherry trifles and set them down on the table. Ryan pushed his chair away and stood up. 'Will you excuse me?' he said. 'I've got a headache——'

'Of course, dear. Are you going upstairs? I'll bring a coffee up——'

'It's all right, Ruth, thanks. I'll be fine soon,' and he walked out.

Adam looked at Beth, his face sad. 'Go on after him, lass,' he said. 'He needs you.'

Beth froze. Oh, no, he doesn't, she thought. But there was no way she could say it. She stood up. 'Of course,' she answered. 'I'll be back.' And she left the two of them together, Ruth knowing, Adam entirely innocent of any undercurrents.

She tapped on Ryan's door. When there was no reply, she went in to see him lying stretched out on top of the bed. He didn't open his eyes. It was as if he knew.

'Go away,' he muttered.

'Adam sent me. He said you needed me.'

'And you and I know that I don't. You've done your duty. Now you go down and tell him I said I'm fine.'

'Do you want anything for your headache?'

'For God's sake, get out!' he burst out. 'If I need anything, I'll get it.'

'There's no need to shout.' Yet she didn't move. His face was deathly white in the light from the bedside lamp, and she could see the sweat beaded on his brow, and his drawn features. This was no mere headache. He was ill. She moved closer to the bed and bent slightly.

'Ryan,' she whispered, 'I'm going to get Ruth——'

His arm shot out and grabbed hers. There was a desperate strength to it, and she winced with pain. 'I—don't—need—anybody,' he gritted, each word an effort. 'Do—you—understand?' His hand dropped away from hers, as if the attempt had been too much, and she heard his shallow breathing, saw the colour of his face, the whiteness of it, and knew she had to do something fast. He opened his eyes and looked at her. 'What are you waiting for?' he said harshly. 'Whatever it is, I'm sorry I won't be able to oblige——' his voice tailed away.

Beth ran out of the room, leaving the door ajar, and down the stairs. Ruth was in the kitchen, and took one look at Beth's face. 'My God, what is it?' she exclaimed.

'You'd better come up and see him. I think he needs the doctor,' Beth answered. They went up again, and

Ruth went over and put her hand on Ryan's forehead. She turned to Beth.

'Go and telephone,' she said. 'Dr Crisp—the number's beside the phone in the library. Tell him it's for Ryan. Tell him he's got a raging temperature—and hurry!'

CHAPTER TEN

It was nearly midnight. The doctor had been gone hours previously, and Ryan slept. Beth, sitting in the kitchen having a much-needed drink of coffee, looked at Ruth.

'I'll stay with him tonight,' she said.

'But there's only the one bed——'

'I'll sleep on the floor if necessary.'

Ruth's face softened. 'Bless you! We've a camp bed somewhere. That'll not take a minute to set up. Are you sure? I can——'

'No, you can't. It's something I've got to do, don't you see?' Beth gazed in anguish at the older woman. 'You have Adam to look after. And I'm younger.'

'I know, love. So be it.' Ruth nodded. 'He'll sleep for a while with any luck now. The doctor gave him a pretty powerful sedative. But if he gets violent, you're to call me.'

'Violent?' whispered Beth.

'In his delirium. He's delirious, don't forget, and they can do funny things during that. If he's no better to-morrow the doctor will get him into hospital, but he thinks he's better here.'

'And you knew—he's had this before, hasn't he?'

Ruth nodded. 'Yes, once. It was some tropical illness he picked up years ago when he was out East—similar to malaria, I imagine. He needs keeping cool, and he needs those pills every four hours. It'll pass in a day or so, it usually does, and Dr Crisp will be in first thing after surgery.' She sighed. 'Poor Beth! You may not get much rest.'

Beth shook her head. 'It doesn't matter. I can doze during the day, when you're there.'

'Of course you can. Best go up now. I'll bring all the flannels and things up in a few minutes.' Beth stood up and went out of the room. She was not aware of the expression on Ruth's face.

She tiptoed in to see Ryan sleeping on his back. He looked quite peaceful, although he was drenched in sweat. Beth gently and carefully wiped his face with the damp flannel she had left there before, then went to put the blankets on her camp bed. Then she pulled up a chair and prepared to sit by his bed for a while, until she was sure he was fast asleep.

Ruth came up, stayed a minute or so, and went. The long night had begun. It started easily enough. After a quarter of an hour Beth went to lie down, fully dressed, and pulled a blanket over her. She listened to Ryan's stertorous breathing, heard the slight murmurs and groans he made from time to time, and gradually drifted off herself into a light sleep. She had shaded the bedside lamp and moved it well away from the bed, leaving it on so that the room was dimly lighted, enough to see by, not enough to disturb sleep.

She was awoken by a crash and sat up to see Ryan struggling to get out of bed. He had knocked all the books from his bedside table, and he was muttering something she couldn't catch. Instantly by his side, she said: 'Easy now, easy, it's all right, Ryan——'

'They're here! We've got to get them——' he glared at her, but she knew he wasn't seeing her. His arm came up and swept her aside. 'I've got to go and sort it out——' She regained her balance and held his arm as he tried to push the bedclothes aside. It needed all her efforts simply to steady his urgent movements, but she managed, because her desperation gave her the added strength she needed.

'I'll get you a drink,' she began. 'You'll feel better——'

'Don't be stupid, woman.' His voice was thick and slurred. 'They've got knives—I don't want a drink——'

It might be better to humour him, and while he was up, escort him to the bathroom. An idea was growing in Beth's mind. One that could make things easier all round. . . .

'The police are here,' she said calmly, 'and they're sorting it out. Come on, we'll go and check for ourselves. Take my arm—I need help too.' She grasped his arm and helped him out of bed, talking, soothing all the while, and they made their way along to her bedroom. 'Go to the bathroom,' she said very firmly, like a mother talking to a stubborn child, 'and while you're there I'll look out of the window and let you know what's happening.' She kept her foot in the door so that he couldn't lock it, then moved nearer the window and called out: 'It's okay, they're leaving now—it's all over!' She pulled the covers down on the bed he had first slept in, and when he came out of the bathroom, guided him to it.

'Sit down, that's it.'

'You don't understand. The place is surrounded——'

'Yes, I *do*. But we've got the dogs now and they're——'

'That's no good. I must——' he fell back, exhausted, and she covered him up, then fled for the damp cloths. She sponged his face and arms, and gradually his muttering subsided. When he was calmer she gave him a pill with water and waited, fingers crossed, for the fever to abate.

He began to breathe more easily after some minutes,

but Beth remained by his side, her hand grasped in his. She felt his fingers tightening on hers. 'Stay with me,' he said.

'Yes, I'll stay.' He suddenly pulled her down beside him on the bed.

'Keep me warm,' he muttered.

'You're warm enough.'

'I'm cold. I'm so cold.'

'All right, I'll keep you warm.' He sighed deeply.

'Have they really gone now?'

'Yes, they've gone.'

'They killed seven, you know—it wasn't nice. I had to do something. I went after them——' his voice tailed away.

'And what did you do?' she asked softly. If he needed to talk, it was better he should. And he was certainly calmer this way.

'I could only get one of them. The others got away. But we made plans, and when they came again the following night, we were waiting for them. We caught them—the police said——' he hesitated as if searching for words.

'Yes. What did the police say?'

'That Marcos Veleta, the leader, was the most wanted man in Argentina.'

The shock of suddenly knowing that what she was hearing was true, and not a figment of a fevered brain, took Beth's breath away completely. She had read of what Ryan was talking about in the newspapers a few years previously, and remembered it only because it had been so horrifying. A gang of bandits had terrorised small mountain villages, robbing and raping—and seemingly too clever to be caught—until the night they had met their match and been caught by an Englishman who had been staying in one of the villages. His name hadn't been mentioned, but his job had—and it fitted.

'My God!' she whispered, shaken. He must have gone out after them, perhaps unarmed, or with only a gun. She had to ask. 'Did you chase after them by yourself?' she asked.

'That first time, yes. Someone had to do something——' his voice tailed away, and she knew that he slept. She lay beside him, he calmer, she in a turmoil of mixed emotions. She had imagined he would be frightened of nothing—she had never thought she would have such drastic proof. After a while she too slept, the sleep of utter exhaustion, and when the light stole in at the windows at dawn she awoke, cramped and stiff, sat up carefully, putting Ryan's arm gently away from her waist, and stood up. She desperately needed a cup of hot strong tea. She watched him for a moment, but he didn't stir, so she crept downstairs and put the kettle on. Then she carried the tea back to her bedroom, leaving the door wide open so that she could hear if Ruth came up. If Ruth should go in his bedroom and see it empty she would get a shock. . . . Beth lay on her bed and closed her eyes for just a few minutes.

When she awoke it was to see Ruth, clad in dressing gown and slippers, standing by her. 'Oh,' said Beth. 'I transferred us here—it seemed easier——'

Ruth smiled. 'Very sensible. How is he?'

Beth pulled a face. 'The night didn't pass without incident.' They were talking in whispers all the time, and she sat up. 'Come on down. I'll tell you what happened.'

She told Ruth quickly while she ate toast in the kitchen, and drank her second cup of tea. 'Phew!' pronounced Ruth when Beth had finished. 'Some story!

At least he told *you*—even if he wasn't aware of it. He would never talk about it to us at all. He got some sort of award from the Argentine government, but he wouldn't even tell us about that. All we ever heard was what we got from the newspapers at the time.'

'I knew it was true when he mentioned that name,' admitted Beth. 'Until then I'd honestly thought it was delirium—and that was a pretty hairy few minutes, I can tell you!'

'You should have called me. I told you——'

'I know. But I thought I could manage, and I did.'

'We'll tell the doctor when he comes. He might transfer him to hospital.'

'No!' said Beth firmly. She felt herself going red, startled at her own vehemence. 'I mean, he's better now, I'm sure of it.'

Ruth tried to hide her little smile but didn't quite succeed. 'You know best,' she agreed calmly.

'It's not that—I——' Beth shook her head. 'Oh!'

They both began to laugh, and Ruth hugged her. 'There, there, *I* understand.'

'I think you do,' agreed Beth.

'Come on, let's see if the invalid wants any breakfast, shall we?' Ruth picked up the tray she had prepared, and they went upstairs.

Ryan was awake. He lay there looking as if he was too weak to move, and smiled faintly. 'Breakfast,' said Ruth. 'Sit up, love.'

Beth helped him to sit up, and pushed an extra pillow behind him. 'What happened?' he asked.

'You had a slight temperature,' said Ruth with delightful understatement. 'But you look heaps better now.'

'I know this is a silly question—but where am I?' It

was an attempt however slight, at humour, which proved something.

'At Witchwood——' Ruth began.

He waved an impatient hand. 'Yes, I know that. But this isn't my bedroom.'

'It's mine,' said Beth. 'I brought you here in the middle of the night. It seemed—easier.'

Ryan took the cup of tea from the tray. His hand trembled. 'Damn,' he muttered.

'It's all right. Drink up and take your pill,' said Ruth briskly. 'The doctor's coming again soon.'

'Again?' he looked blank.

Ruth looked at Beth, one eyebrow lifted slightly. 'Never mind,' she soothed. 'Here you are.' She handed him the yellow capsule.

He looked at it as he might have looked at a time-bomb. 'There's something you're not telling me.' He gave Ruth a look of desperate appeal. 'What *happened*?'

'I think you had an attack of fever of some kind. Don't you remember?'

'Oh God,' he groaned, and closed his eyes. 'Not that bloody thing again!'

'Everything's under control.' Ruth handed him a plate of toast. 'Try and have some.'

'Was I awful?'

Beth said, with the greatest possible tact, 'I think I've left something in the kitchen——' and drifted out. She heard Ruth's voice as she left. Then she ran down the stairs. She didn't really know why she had gone, except that she sensed he might prefer her not to be there when Ruth told him the truth. She waited downstairs until she heard Ruth's footsteps, and opened the kitchen door. 'Did you tell him?'

'I gave him a watered-down version. He knows you spent the night with him.'

'Oh. And what did he say to that?'

'He—er—seemed confused.'

Yes, he would be, thought Beth wryly. 'He seems much better,' she said. 'That's something.'

'He is—this morning. But these things take a day or so. Are you sure you're up to it? I mean, the doctor is very co-operative——'

'Yes, I know, but——' Beth shrugged. 'It's all right.'

'Why, Beth?'

'Because——' Beth looked at the older woman who was so kind, so understanding. 'It's just because I have to do—to look after him. Don't ask me *why*, because I don't really know myself.' Her eyes were bright with tears.

'Is it because you love him?' asked Ruth very softly.

There was a long, long pause. 'Yes.'

'Ah.' Ruth looked so wise at that moment. 'It shines out of you. Be careful. Don't let him hurt you.'

'I'll try not to.' Beth gave a wry smile. 'I know—I accept he's a loner, an adventurer if you like. It doesn't change my feelings. We don't choose who we fall in love with. If we did, I'd have no problems. I've several interesting men friends, but——' she shrugged, 'that's all I want them to be. Friends. No man has ever had the effect on me that he has. I would go to the ends of the earth for him. But he despises me.' She sat down and put her head in her hands. 'I know what he thinks of me——'

'How do you know?'

Beth shook her head. 'It would take too long to tell. Let's just say the sparks fly whenever we bump into one another. Haven't you felt it? The tension when we're both in the same room? Oh, we make the effort when Adam's there, but the undercurrents are there all the time.'

'Oh yes, I've been aware of those all right. I'd be stupid not to be. But when he heard you call—*thought* he heard you call,' Ruth corrected herself, 'the other night, it wasn't as if he despised you.'

'I'm—I'm not sure what you mean,' Beth began doubtfully.

'I saw his face. I remember his expression——' Ruth stopped.

'Yes? Go on.'

'It was—oh, I can't put it into words. Strange——'

'Strange in what way?'

But Ruth rubbed her forehead, frowning. 'Just—odd. As if—as if he were a man going to meet his love.'

Ruth wasn't cruel. She was never cruel, but her words tore at Beth's heart. 'No,' said Beth. 'No. if you'd seen him when he met me—you wouldn't have said that.'

'Then I was wrong. I'm sorry, Beth.' Ruth managed a smile. 'I shouldn't have said that. How stupid he is, how very stupid.'

'I'd better go back.' Beth stood up, and swayed with tiredness. Ruth caught her arm.

'I'll look after him——'

'No. You have Adam. I'll be all right. I'll have a rest later, when the doctor's been.' Beth walked out slowly, and went up the stairs.

Ryan lay back, eyes closed. He opened them when Beth went in. 'Thank you,' he said.

'What for? Looking after you? I'd have done the same for a stray dog,' she answered. 'I'll get you some water for a wash.' And she picked up one of the plastic bowls that held damp flannels and took it into the bathroom.

Beth had seen enough films and television programmes on nursing to know nurses behaved. Crisp, efficient— impersonal. What was the expression sometimes used? TLC? Tender, loving care. Ryan would get the care all right, and she would be concerned, but love and tender- ness were going to be out of it. If it was so obvious to Ruth. . . .

'Sit up—that's it.' She soaped the flannel and handed it to him. 'Can you manage or shall I wash you?'

'I can manage. Can I have my razor?'

'Certainly. Where is it?' Crisp, impersonal, even brisk.

'Top of my chest of drawers—next to my toothbrush.'

'Very well.' She nodded and went out.

Fifteen minutes later he was washed, shaved, and looking fractionally better, but still white-faced and lying back, clearly tired with the effort of washing himself. Beth cleared away the bowl, then went back into the bedroom and stood at the foot of his bed. 'Anything else you need,' she asked, 'before I go and wash and change? The doctor will be here soon.'

'No thanks.'

She began to gather her possessions together. 'I'll use the other bathroom,' she told him. Did she sound too crisp? It didn't matter. 'Then you can rest.' Before he could answer, she went out of the room. When she re- turned some twenty minutes later, it was to see him sprawled on the floor by the bed. Her heart leaped into her throat. Flinging her towel and toilet bag to one side, she went and knelt by his side. 'Ryan—oh, Ryan!'

He looked up groggily. 'I fell—went to bathroom— lost my balance——'

'Don't try and talk. Let me help you into bed.' He was extremely heavy, she realised a moment later, as she managed to secure a good grip under his arms. Then with all her strength, he trying to assist her, she got him to the side of the bed. From there it was easier. Ryan pulled himself up and fell in. Beth covered him up and stood looking down at him. Grey-faced, he looked back at her, perhaps not really seeing her. 'The doctor might think it better if you go into hospital——' she began, frightened lest he fall and injure himself.

'*No!*' he cut in. 'I've never been in hospital and I'm not going to go now——'

'Sshh! Let me get you a drink. You've to have plenty of liquids, he said. We'll see what he thinks——'

'I can manage,' he gritted, temper sparking. At least it was a sign of life. She passed him a glass of water and he drank some. 'Thanks.' She put her hand on his forehead, and the heat of it frightened her. 'Tell me,' he demanded, 'I can see by your face I've got a raging temperature, haven't I?'

'You're certainly not cool,' she retorted. 'But then you've not lost your usual aggression. That can only be a good sign.' She wrung out a flannel and laid it across his brow. A flicker of a smile touched his lips.

'You make a good nurse.'

'I do my best,' she retorted smartly.

He groaned. 'God, I'm tired. But when I close my eyes I get such awful pictures, it's better to keep them open.'

'Then I'll stay and talk to you. I can have a rest later.'

'Did I keep you awake all night?'

'No. I managed some sleep.'

'Was I rough on you?'

She smiled. 'You couldn't help it. You were delirious.'

'What was I talking about?'

'Oh. I didn't get much sense out of it,' she lied. 'You're talking perfectly rationally now. So you're probably over the worst.'

'I'm as weak as a kitten. I hate that.'

'It must be a change for you,' she answered dryly. 'But until you've recovered, there's not a lot you can do about it. Now, I'll go and get the newspapers and read to you if you like.'

'No, don't go.'

She looked at him, surprised. 'You want me to stay?'

He closed his eyes. 'I—want you to stay.' He made it sound as though he had had a confession wrung from him. Beth sat down demurely on her bed.

'Then *I'll* read,' she said, picked up one of her books and opened it. There was silence for several minutes. She wasn't aware of what she was reading, but she certainly wouldn't admit it to him. The words made no sense. She was far too finely tuned to his mood. He lay back, eyes open, looking at the ceiling, and the grey smudges of fatigue beneath his eyes were a pain in her heart.

'Why did you offer to look after me?' he asked after a while.

Beth had thought about that one to herself. The answer was beautifully simple. 'You looked after me well when we were stuck in the snow at the cottage,' she answered, 'So this is the least I can do in return.'

There was a further silence while he digested the words. One thing has changed, she thought. There's no longer the prickly, aggressive atmosphere when we're alone. When *that* came back, she would know he had recovered.

There was a distant ringing at the doorbell, and she closed the book. 'That will be the doctor,' she said.

'Don't tell him I fell,' said Ryan quickly.

'What? Of course I——'

'Please, Beth.'

Ryan, pleading? It was almost too much.

'But I——'

'Please. It was stupid of me to get up alone. I thought I was strong enough. I won't do it again.'

'All right. But it's your temperature that's more important. You can't lie about that.'

'I know. I'll abide by what he says.' He lay back exhausted. And they waited for Dr Crisp to come up.

The doctor had quite obviously never had a patient like Ryan before. He stood out of earshot of the bedroom with Ruth and Beth, and gave them his opinion.

'He's a tough one,' he said, shaking his head. 'Anyone else and I'd have whipped them off to hospital last night, but he—well,' he shrugged, 'he's different. Difficult—but certainly different. How are you coping?'

'Very well,' Beth answered. 'He does as he's told. He had a bad half hour during the night when he was delirious, but I calmed him down and he slept well after that.'

'Don't go tiring yourself now,' the doctor admonished her. 'You get a rest today. He'll be poorly for a couple of days, but he's got the constitution of an ox. Keep him comfortable, get as much nourishing drink down him as you can and forget about food if he's not interested.' He began to write on his prescription pad, tore it off and handed it to Beth, then wrote some things down on the back of an envelope and handed that to her. 'When you go to the chemist, get these things as well. They're a bit pricey, but they give them in hospital to patients who can't take solid food. I'll call in tomorrow and see him. Take care now.' To Ruth, he said, 'I might as well have a look at Adam while I'm here. Where is he?'

'This way, doctor.' Ruth led him away, and Beth went back to the bedroom.

'What was he whispering about?' demanded Ryan.

'Couldn't you hear? He said you were going on nicely and had to do exactly what you're told. That should make a change for you.'

'You're supposed to be looking after me, not lecturing me,' he said.

Beth raised her eyebrows. 'Hmm, getting a bit of life back, are we? That's good!' She smoothed down his pillows. 'I'm going for your prescription soon—and some invalid food.' She gave him a gentle smile. 'You'll like that.'

'I'm sure I'll love it,' he responded sarcastically. 'I'd rather have steak and chips.'

'Then you shall have, if that's what you want.' She kicked off her slippers and found her shoes. 'As soon as Ruth comes back, I'll go.' She put the papers in her handbag.

'Look, get my wallet, will you? I can't let you pay for everything.'

'We can sort that out later. You're not well enough to think about money yet.'

'I will be tomorrow. I'll be up and about tomorrow.'

She looked at him steadily. 'Don't be foolish. You're nowhere near——'

'Want to bet?'

'I don't make bets on silly things like that. You're too weak to——'

'You don't know me very well, do you?'

'Well enough.' Her tone was very dry.

'And I mean what I say. I'll throw this bug off, whatever it is. I'm feeling much better now——'

'You felt well enough to go to the bathroom on your own, and look what happened——'

'Damn it!' he snapped, cutting her off effectively by the force of his tone. 'I *will* be up tomorrow.'

And, looking at him, Beth thought—I'll just bet you will. 'You won't if you waste all your energy arguing,' she said swiftly.

He subsided instantly as if he knew the sense of her words. Then he smiled. The smile had a touch—just a touch—of the old, aggressive Ryan about it. 'You're right. But I'll show you.'

'I hope you do. Then maybe I can have my bedroom back.' And she smiled ever so sweetly at him. It was nice having the upper hand, just for once. She could hear Ruth returning.

'I'm going now. I'll get you some steak—as well as those other things, of course. We have to obey the doctor, don't we?'

'Yes, Matron.'

She was laughing when Ruth came in. 'He's all yours,' she told her. 'Watch him, he's nearly back on form again.' And she left a bemused Ruth staring at Ryan. She ran down the stairs and went to get Adam's car out. Matron, he had called her. All right, she thought, as she went down the drive, you'll see how matron-like I can be! There was a certain piquancy to the situation. Today could well prove an interesting one. What was it the doctor had said? 'He's difficult—but certainly different.' That he was. Different from any man she had ever known in her life. And difficult—oh yes, he was that all right. But today, he was going to behave himself. Tomorrow could take care of itself. Beth changed gear and sped along the road. She didn't feel tired at all any more. It was as though a challenge had been issued, and she had accepted it.

CHAPTER ELEVEN

'DRINK this,' said Beth.

Ryan looked stonily at the beaker she proffered. 'I'm not having that rubbish,' he said. 'Where's my steak?'

'How do you like your steak done? Rare—medium—crisp?'

'Medium.'

'Good. I also bought some button mushrooms to go with it. And when you've drunk all your *lovely* invalid drink then I'll think about going down and doing your lovely steak.'

It was clear that a battle was going on inside him. There was a brief but pregnant silence, then he took the beaker from her. 'Every drop now,' said Beth, 'or——'

'I don't get my steak. You should have a record made, it'll save you repeating it.' He drank, his eyes pained, and Beth inspected the empty cup.

'That's good.' She stood up and went to the door. 'I'll be back in fifteen minutes. Get your bib ready.' She was out of the room before he could reply.

She had bought enough steak and mushrooms for the four of them, and told Ruth she would prepare the lunch. It was going to be absolutely perfect. He wanted his steak medium, that was how he would get it. Ruth prepared the potatoes while Beth made her own preparations. She had always enjoyed cooking, but until now, at Witchwood, had had little opportunity.

Ruth watched her at work. 'You're enjoying yourself, aren't you?'

'I am. And one word of complaint from him and he'll get the plate tipped up over his head.'

'I don't think he'd dare,' laughed Ruth. 'He's obviously better, but still not himself. I mentioned about the typing when you'd left—let's face it, it seemed the perfect opportunity to get some work done now he's off his feet, and I told him you'd probably do some typing while you were here, because you enjoyed keeping your mind active, and do you know what he said?'

'What?'

'He said "I think you're mistaken—I wouldn't ask her." And do you know, he looked like a little lost boy when he said it.'

'Huh!' snorted Beth.

'No. True—he did.'

Beth paused. Perhaps he had. 'His bout of fever has certainly knocked some of the stuffing out of him,' she said. 'I'll sort it out when I take this up. If I'm staying with him I might as well do something useful—I certainly can't concentrate on a book.' She looked at the older woman. '*He* says he'll be up and fit tomorrow.'

'I shouldn't be at all surprised.'

'Nor should I,' Beth admitted. 'Golly, but he's a tough one!'

'You can say that again!'

They had a quick cup of tea while the chips bubbled, and the steak and mushrooms sizzled gently away, and then all was ready. Beth carried up the large tray and went into the bedroom. 'Sit up,' she said.

Ryan sat up, he looked, and he went: 'Mmm,' drawing in a deep breath, 'I could smell that from along the corridor. I'm starving!'

'Then here it is.' She balanced her own plate on her knee and started eating.

'Did you cook this yourself?'

She looked up sharply. One wrong word—— 'Yes.'

'It's superb.'

'There's no need to overdo it,' she said calmly. But she was well pleased. 'About this typing you wanted doing,' she said. There were occasions when it was best to plunge in head first, before you had time to think properly. 'I can do some up here while I'm invalid sitting.'

'I would appreciate it, but——'

'Then it's settled. It's extremely boring for me to do nothing, I assure you. We'll get things sorted out when you've eaten.'

'You must let me know the correct rate for the job.'

'Of course. I'm doing it for the money, not love.' The last two words, softly said, fell into the air and vanished —but they had been heard, she knew that.

She assisted him to get out of bed when he had eaten, and into the bathroom. 'I'll go and find the typewriter,' she said. 'Don't try being clever and getting into bed on your own, I'll not be a minute.'

But when she returned he was sitting up in bed, only the whiteness of his face betraying the effort. She stared at him. 'I told you——'

'I know. I'm much stronger now. I'll tell you where my notes are.' Beth put the portable typewriter and box of paper on the table by the window, then waited for him to tell her.

When she returned with his notes she put them beside the typewriter. 'I'll work better if I lie down for ten minutes first,' she told him. 'I suggest you have a rest as well.' So saying, she took off her slippers and lay on top of her bed. Five minutes later she was fast asleep.

It was nearly dark when she woke and she didn't know

where she was. Then, remembering, she looked round in panic. Ryan lay in bed watching her. She sat up, confused.

'Why didn't you wake me?' she demanded.

'Because you were tired out, you obviously needed the sleep, and because I didn't want anything.'

She stood up, shaky-legged, then sat down. 'Oof!' she exclaimed. 'I'm not used to sleeping during the day.'

'Nor am I,' he answered dryly, 'but I must have slept as well. I've only just come round myself.' She switched on the soft wall lights and the shadows vanished.

'I'll start the typing,' she said. 'Anything I don't get I can ask you about. Are you sure the noise of the typewriter won't disturb you?'

'No.'

She went and sat down, flexing her fingers. Then she put the paper in the machine and began to type from the first page of his notes. His handwriting was upright and decisive and very easy to read. Gradually she became absorbed in what she was doing, and only the staccato rattle of the typewriter keys filled the room. A slight noise made her turn her head, and—— 'Ah!' she nearly jumped out of her seat to see Ryan standing almost beside her.

'I'm sorry. I was going to the bathroom. I didn't want to disturb you——'

'You damned near gave me a heart attack!' she exclaimed, her heart bumping violently against her ribs. 'Anyway, if you were going to the bathroom what are you standing here for?'

'I wanted to see how far you'd got. You're very fast.'

'I know. I also don't make mistakes—unless people creep up behind me.' She stood up and took his arm. 'Come on, off you go.' And, quite suddenly, she knew he was much better, because the tension filled the room. Her heart, which had been steadying down, began to bump again. She looked up at him, and saw what was in his eyes, and said weakly: 'You can't stand here all——'

'I don't need your help. I can manage.'

His arm burned hers, so she took hers away. 'Then manage,' she whispered, and watched him go. She ran blindly out of the room, her body trembling and shaky at the brief encounter. Then, standing in the corridor to calm herself, she waited for strength to return.

When she went back he was sitting up in bed reading the pages she had typed.

'I'm going down to make myself a drink,' she said. 'I'll bring you one.'

'Tea, please. Not that mush you——'

'You'll get what you're given. You can hand out your orders when you're better,' she answered sharply, turned on her heel, and went out. She thought she heard him laughing, but it might have been her imagination.

After dinner she stayed downstairs with her grandfather for a while, chatting, and when it was time for him to go to bed, she kissed his cheek warmly. Then she went upstairs.

'Where have you been?' he asked. She stared at him.

'I *beg* your pardon?'

'You've been gone ages.'

'So I have! I brought you your dinner up, didn't I? I've had a talk with Adam. You've been telling me how much better you are. I didn't really think I'd be missed.'

'It's damned boring up here on my own.'

'Is it now? You must be feeling *much* better, then—or you wouldn't be bored.' She sat down on his bed. 'Do you need entertaining? I can read to you, or you can have the portable TV up here, Ruth says, while I get on with that typing.'

'I'll have the TV—then you can go and do what you want to,' he retorted. 'Do forgive me—I'm quite sure you're also bored stiff stuck up here with me.'

'Don't be childish,' she answered, and turned her head away. 'I said I'd look after you, and I'm going to. But don't make it more difficult for yourself.'

'Your job will be over tomorrow.'

'So you keep saying. But you'd feel better if you were more sweet-tempered,' she shot back. 'The doctor was right. He said you were difficult, and you are!' She glared at him. The colour was returning to his face, the life to his eyes. You have to hand it to him, she thought, he's determined enough to *make* himself better by morning. She leaned over to plump up his pillows. 'Sit up,' she ordered, and he did so. But instead of lying back when she had finished, he caught hold of her and took her with him.

'What do you think you're——' she began, gasping. He was certainly stronger!

'Don't worry, it's not catching,' he said softly, pulled her tightly to him, and kissed her. She jerked herself away from him, red-cheeked, breathless.

She stood up. 'I won't ask you what that was for,' she said. 'But don't do it again.'

'But I'll tell you anyway. For the superb nursing skill and sheer bossiness——'

'Don't spoil it. You could have stopped at the nursing bit. I told you already, I'd have done the same for a sick dog.' And she smiled, now she was a safe distance, and had her confidence back. 'And I'll tell you something else. You don't need *me* sleeping in the room with *you*, any more.'

Ryan lay back and closed his eyes. 'I feel ill,' he said faintly.

'No, you don't. You don't fool me. I'm moving out this evening—I'll sleep in your old room. You can stay here with your own bathroom. I'll listen out for you.' She went to the door. 'I'll bring up the television now. Then perhaps you'll stop moaning about being bored.' And out she went.

It was impossible for her to type in the same room, she discovered, because it made the programme difficult to hear. She put the cover on the typewriter, stacked the papers neatly, and went and told him, 'I'm going. I'll call in later to see if there's anything you need.' She glanced across at the portable colour television which was showing a taut detective thriller, then she walked out.

It was later that she went up quietly, carrying a cup of Horlicks for Ryan. The television was on, the door ajar. She pushed it open, then gasped in surprise at what she saw. 'Ryan!'

He turned guiltily, stood up, and said: 'I was only——'

'I can see what you were doing, thank you. You're supposed to be in bed watching television, not weight-lifting.' Beth went over, handed him the beaker, and lifted away the chair, weighted with books, that he had been lifting over his head.

'I'm getting my strength back.'

'Killing yourself, more like,' she retorted. 'Please get into bed. Here's your Horlicks.'

'Thank you, nurse.'

'Have I been demoted? It was Matron this morning.'

'That was before you started typing. Matrons don't type.'

'All right,' she said wearily. 'There's nothing wrong with your tongue, anyway.'

She watched him drink, marvelling at the speed of his recovery. Weak and delirious one minute, lifting and balancing book loaded chairs the next. Then she took the beaker from him. 'Goodnight,' she said.

'Goodnight.' She walked out and closed the door.

The following morning Ryan was dressed when she went in, standing by the window looking out. He turned as Beth opened the door. 'I'm hungry,' he said, 'and I'm coming down for breakfast.'

She shrugged. 'As you wish.' She turned and went out, down the stairs and into the kitchen. Ruth was grilling bacon, singing cheerfully as she broke eggs into a pan. 'The patient will be down any minute,' Beth told her.

'Good gracious!' Ruth turned. 'He meant it!'

'He was weightlifting last night. What else can you expect?'

'Mmm, an extra egg for him, I think,' laughed Ruth.

'I'm going to the village today—may I borrow Adam's car?'

'Of course, love.'

'Anything I can get you?'

'Oh—well, one or two things. Can I give you a list afterwards?'

'Of course.' Beth sat at the table. 'Is it the village where the other Beth lived?'

'It is. The cottage she lived in has long gone, of course, but the cemetery——' she stopped.

'Yes?' Beth was puzzled.

'Oh—nothing, really. I was just going to say that they buried her sweetheart in the cemetery just outside the village—you'll pass it on your way in, but you wouldn't be interested——'

'I'd like to see it. What was his name?'

'Ben Smith. The grave is just by the gate. Funnily enough it's always in good condition, as though someone cares for it. Never any weeds or grass, you know.'

'Perhaps it's Beth's ghost,' said Beth lightly—then stopped. A shiver had gone through her.

Ruth laughed. 'Ah, maybe.' Then Ryan came into the kitchen. He walked in slowly, and he looked as if he had just run two miles instead of making his way down the stairs—but he had done it. Which was precisely what he had been determined to do. He sat down and Ruth looked at him. 'You're a bad lad,' she scolded. 'I don't know what the doctor will say.'

Ryan smiled. 'Probably be delighted to lose a patient, my dear Ruth. And I'm hungry enough to eat a horse.'

'Bacon and eggs is what you'll get, though. And take your time over it. Then you can go in and wait for Adam to come down. He's missed you—though Beth's been looking after him very well.' She smiled at him fondly as she handed him his plate, and they all began to eat.

Beth left the village shortly afterwards. It was a glorious October day, with a fine ground mist, promising warmth to come, and the snow had nearly gone altogether. She followed Ruth's directions and found the village—not the one they had passed through on the way there, but another, smaller and more compact, with all the houses of grey stone, and a long street of shops. Just before she reached it she saw the cemetery, on a gentle slope leading up to an old church. She stopped the car outside and sat for a few minutes, looking over the rolling Derbyshire hills that stretched away on either side, the higher ones still streaked with snow. All was quiet. She got out and opened the wooden lych gate and walked in slowly.

She saw the grave near the gate. A simple stone bore

the inscription 'Ben Smith, son of Benjamin and Dorcas Smith. 1792. At rest.'

The grave was neatly tended, as were indeed all the others, but there was something more, something slightly different about this one which Beth couldn't put her finger on. It did indeed look more cared for. She stood for a moment looking at it. A lump was in her throat, a sadness she felt as strongly as if she had known him. He had waited every night for Beth Linden to return, only she never had. He had kept his lonely vigil in the woods, seeking, searching, calling her name—until the night when he had found her. And Beth knew, suddenly, that she would never be afraid of the woods after dark again. Because there was nothing to fear. Whatever sadness had once been was gone.

It was time for her to leave. She looked at her watch and discovered to her surprise that twenty minutes had passed, yet she felt as if she had been standing there for only moments. There was a great sense of calmness within her as she turned and walked away, closing the creaky gate behind her, getting into the car, and driving on towards the village.

She did her shopping, and that for Ruth, and returned to Witchwood well before lunch. She could hear Adam and Ryan talking as she passed the lounge, so she opened the door and looked in.

'I'm going to finish polishing in the chapel,' she told them, 'and then I'll do some typing after lunch if you'll get the notes ready that you want doing.' This last addressed to Ryan.

'Fine. I will.' He smiled at her—strictly for Adam's benefit, she knew, but it didn't stop her heart bumping erratically. 'The doctor's been.'

'Oh. What did he say?'

'More or less gave me a good ticking off—didn't he, Adam?' Ryan grinned at her grandfather, who nodded, chuckling. 'And then he said he wouldn't be seeing me again, he'd better things to do than waste his time visiting people who didn't need him.'

'That's good.' Beth beamed, as if in relief. 'But don't think you can stop taking your pills, my sweet, it's a five-day course of antibiotics and however well you feel you have to finish them. So I'll go and get them for you.' And she gave him a loving smile and went out.

She couldn't help hearing Adam's words as the door closed. 'Ah, she's a good lass, Ryan. You're a lucky man.' She fled up the stairs. She didn't want to hear Ryan's reply—if any.

After lunch was over, she went into the library with the typewriter and sat by the window, from where she could see the woods, and began to type. It was dark when Ryan came in, and Beth had on the angled table lamp, which shone in a brilliant yellow pool on the table, leaving the rest of the room in shadow. She didn't hear the door open, so engrossed was she in what she was doing, and she jumped when he said: 'Dinner's nearly ready.'

'My God, I do wish——'

'I'm sorry.' He was close behind her now, too close for her comfort, and she felt stifled. She had scarcely spoken to him after lunch, only once when she had a query about the spelling of a place name in Crete, and all her concentration had been on the work she was doing. He rested his hands on the back of her chair. She could feel the pressure of them.

'I hope you remembered to take your pills,' she said. She wanted to move away, but could not.

'I did—Adam reminded me. We've been talking.'

'Have you? Excuse me, can I get——'

'About you.'

She was very still. His presence was overwhelming to her, standing there, solid, immovable, a constant threat to her peace of mind, physically and emotionally disturbing to her.

'Aren't you going to ask me what we said?'

'No. You've been talking about me. I don't want to know—any more.' His fingers brushed the back of her neck, and it was like an electric current touching her. 'Please,' she whispered. 'Please—don't.'

'I think he knows,' said Ryan.

'That we're not—not married?'

'Not that, no.'

'Then——' the words could not be said. She wanted to turn, to stand, to be crushed in his arms, for comfort and warmth—but she couldn't have moved, not for the world.

'I think you must talk to him after dinner. Then perhaps you'll see, and perhaps, if the time is right—and you will know if it is——'

'He showed me a photo of his first wife the other day. He said she looked very much like me—and it was true.' Beth put her hands on the table, as if that would give her the strength she needed. She was feeling dizzy. And she didn't feel hungry, at all. 'I've got to think,' she said. 'Please let me think.'

'Of course. I thought I would prepare you. It won't be a shock to him—I know that now, for I've seen what was in his eyes when he spoke about you.' Ryan moved away, and she was able to get up, to turn around to face him.

'I'm going out for a walk to clear my head,' she said. She couldn't remain in the same room with him any longer, and she couldn't touch food.

'It's nearly dinner time——'

'Then start without me. I'm not hungry.'

He stood there looking at her, just looking at her, and she couldn't bear it any longer. 'Aren't you well?'

Aren't you well—the same way that he might say, it's warm outside—couldn't he *see*? Was he blind?

'I'm absolutely fine,' she said, and brushed past him. Her coat was on the monk's bench in the hall, where she had left it, intending to put it away later. She picked it up and put it on and went outside, closing the heavy front door behind her. She turned briefly as she walked away from the house, and saw a white blur of a face at the library window, and she ached with the love for him. A useless, hopeless love. There was only one place she wanted to walk to—Witchwood. She sought the comfort of the woods, the place that would never frighten her again, not since that morning, a place where she could be alone and think about everything, about her grandfather, and what she might tell him, and about Ryan. Because once her grandfather knew the truth, really knew instead of guessing, she could go away for a while until Ryan himself had gone.

She walked into the trees, into the dark shadows, and they swallowed her up. The love which had once been, over a century ago, reached out to enfold her, to soothe her.

The mist of the morning had returned, a faint haze swirling round her legs and feet, slightly cold but with nothing to fear of it. She went deeper, and now, away from the house, she could think more clearly. Twigs and dead leaves crunched underfoot and the woods were filled with a waiting, a listening, as if the trees that had once heard Ben's voice calling to his sweetheart would hear his voice again, and know.

The moon's light filtered through the trees, and she walked more quickly now, as if escaping from something. Escaping from Ryan. She heard the whispering from above, but it was only a light breeze, moving the leafless branches, not reaching the ground, where the gauze of the mist lent a softness to the surroundings. The woods had a magic that was all their own.

She saw the old bench under the tree, didn't see it until she nearly fell over it. Ruth had told her about it once, briefly. It had been there for years and years, she said. It might have been there when Beth and Ben came. It might have been their meeting place, no one knew, certainly not Ruth. Beth sat down and leaned against the solid bark behind her. Would anyone ever know why the other Beth had disappeared so many years ago? Perhaps it was better they shouldn't, because there would always be this air of enchantment—of mystery. She was no witch, of that Beth was certain, just a girl, born before her time. She breathed in the night-scented air, and a certain calmness came upon her, the calm she had been seeking when she left the house.

She could picture the wood in springtime, with the buds bursting open on the trees, and the grass growing thick and luxuriant, and the sleeping daffodils awakening, and she could picture the two young lovers meeting, and saying the things—the same things—that lovers have said since the beginning of time, the whispering, the kisses, the sitting there and simply holding hands while the shadows lengthened, and the wood became darker, and it was their own world, where only they belonged.

The tears blurred her eyes, and the trees shimmered and danced in them, and she knew she could stay there for ever—but must not. She didn't want to leave, not yet. She was possessed by the magic, she was part of the spell that the woods wove round anyone who entered them, and she had been too blind to see before, but now her eyes were opened. Then she opened them literally, and saw, coming towards her through the mist, a man.

The man was Ryan. She watched him silently, and he came to her and sat down beside her on the bench, and took her hands. 'You're cold,' he said softly.

'Yes. How did you know I was here?'

'How did I know? I knew, that's all. You've been gone over an hour.'

'No, I've only been——' An hour? She had been here only minutes, surely?

'It's nearly half past eight. You were gone—I knew you were scared——'

'Not any more. There's nothing frightening here.' She realised that he was still holding her hands, but there seemed nothing odd about it. It seemed exactly right. Then he moved, ever so slightly, only a whisper nearer, but enough.

'I love you, Beth,' he said.

'I know. I love you too.' She turned to look at him, and he enfolded her in his arms, and kissed her. After the kiss was over—a beautiful, very satisfying kiss that said it all—she began to laugh.

'We're mad,' she said.

'That too,' he agreed. 'Mad to have spent all this time fighting each other, instead of making love. And although, in a way, I've known it all along, I didn't admit it to myself until you walked out of the library tonight and I saw you walking down the drive, away from the house, and I went to find Ruth and tell her about dinner—and she took one look at my face and asked me what had happened, and I told her. And do you know what she said?'

'No. What did she say?'

'She said, "About time too. I've wanted to bang your heads together many a time!"' Beth listened, totally without surprise. Her capacity for being surprised had vanished the moment she had seen Ryan walking towards her, because she too had known the truth of it all in that instant of time.

'I thought I would never know happiness again,' he said softly, holding her closely so that she would not be cold. 'I thought I was a loner. I was wrong. I want you—I love you more dearly than life itself.'

'And I you,' she murmured. 'I want to be with you——'

'You will be. Always.' He stroked her cheek gently. 'I think—there'll have to be a double wedding in the chapel.'

'But—my grandfather? How——'

'Gently, very gently—we can tell him. I know that now.' Ryan sighed and looked up at the tall trees. 'There's something about these woods——'

'I know what it is. Why do you think I'm no longer frightened?'

And somewhere in the distance, they seemed to hear faint laughter, the happy laughter of a child, or of a young woman who is going to meet her lover.

 Harlequin

COLLECTION
EDITIONS OF 1978

Harlequin's Collection 1?
ANDREA BLAKE
Night of the Hurrica

Harlequin's Collection 106   1.25
ANNE WEALE
If This Is Love

**50 great stories
of special beauty
and significance**

$1.25
each novel

In 1976 we introduced the first 100 Harlequin Collections—a selection of titles chosen from our best sellers of the past 20 years. This series, a trip down memory lane, proved how great romantic fiction can be timeless and appealing from generation to generation. The theme of love and romance is eternal, and, when placed in the hands of talented, creative, authors whose true gift lies in their ability to write from the heart, the stories reach a special level of brilliance that the passage of time cannot dim. Like a treasured heirloom, an antique of superb craftsmanship, a beautiful gift from someone loved—these stories too, have a special significance that transcends the ordinary. **$1.25 each novel**

Here are your 1978
Harlequin Collection Editions...

Original Harlequin Romance numbers in brackets

ORDER FORM
Harlequin Reader Service

In U.S.A.
MPO Box 707
Niagara Falls, N.Y. 14302

In Canada
649 Ontario St.,
Stratford, Ontario, N5A 6W2

Please send me the following Harlequin Collection novels. I am enclosing my check or money order for $1.25 for each novel ordered, plus 25¢ to cover postage and handling.

☐ 102	☐ 115	☐ 128	☐ 140
☐ 103	☐ 116	☐ 129	☐ 141
☐ 104	☐ 117	☐ 130	☐ 142
☐ 105	☐ 118	☐ 131	☐ 143
☐ 106	☐ 119	☐ 132	☐ 144
☐ 107	☐ 120	☐ 133	☐ 145
☐ 108	☐ 121	☐ 134	☐ 146
☐ 109	☐ 122	☐ 135	☐ 147
☐ 110	☐ 123	☐ 136	☐ 148
☐ 111	☐ 124	☐ 137	☐ 149
☐ 112	☐ 125	☐ 138	☐ 150
☐ 113	☐ 126	☐ 139	☐ 151
☐ 114	☐ 127		

Number of novels checked @
$1.25 each = $ _____
N.Y. and N.J. residents add
appropriate sales tax $ _____

Postage and handling $ ___.25

                               TOTAL $ _____

NAME _____

ADDRESS _____
(Please Print)

CITY _____

STATE/PROV. _____

ZIP/POSTAL CODE _____

AB   ROM 2245

Offer expires June 30, 1979

And there's still *more* love in

Harlequin Presents...